EXPERIENCE PIPELINE

Experience Pipeline

by Quinn Haber

Casagrande Press • Solana Beach, California

Published by Casagrande Press
Solana Beach, California

www.casagrandepress.com
casagrandepress@aol.com

Copy Editor: Steve Connell
Book Design: Ryan Mcfarlane - www.liminal.biz
Cover and inside photos: Sean Davey
Inside photo: Derek Ho surfing Pipeline in 1994.

Printed in Canada
Haber, Quinn, 1968-
Experience Pipeline / by Quinn Haber.
p. cm.
Summary: The reader is placed at the Pipe Masters surfing contest in
Oahu, Hawaii, where the story progresses based on the results of a coin-
flip at the bottom of each page.
ISBN 0-9769516-3-0

1. Plot-your-own stories. [1. Surfing--Fiction. 2. Contests--Fiction. 3.
Hawaii--Fiction. 4. Plot-your-own stories.] I. Title.

PZ7.H14424Ex 2008
[Fic]--dc22

2007041086

This book is dedicated to you. May life's adventures grant you folly, experience, and wisdom.

Contents

Introduction

Surfing's greatest and most anticipated contest is the Pipe Masters event, which happens every winter on the North Shore of Oahu when the waves get big enough. There's nothing more exciting than watching the world's best surfers compete not only with each other, but—more significantly—with the challenging and hazardous wave itself. At Pipeline huge and powerful waves break over a frighteningly shallow reef. Perfect rides or career-ending wipeouts happen with alarming frequency at this world-class break. On this heavy and fast moving court the bravest don't always get the best rides, the most skilled surfers don't always make their wave, and the more cautious surfers can find themselves facing full-throttle disaster in the blink of an eye. Winning the Pipe Masters event takes skill, cunning, bravado, and luck.

The Pipe Masters event is provocative to witness. The shaking ground and booming percussion of the surf is as close to the action as most surfers will come. In fact, fewer than one in a million surfers will ever get to experience the contest. Until now, there was no way to know and feel what it's like to be out there competing under the pressures of pride, opponents, sponsors, and the wave itself. Even some of the best grade-A pros never get a chance to experience the contest. But now you do. You are holding the experience in your hands, and the experience is waiting for you.

This book places you directly in the lineup at the start of the contest. And true to the Pipe Masters event there is no predetermination, no fait accompli; there is only intense action and, in the end, victory or defeat. Get ready for the firsthand immediacy and randomness of a big-wave competition. This book delivers hundreds of possible plots and endings as your contest unfolds by the chance flip of a coin.

Quinn Haber
North Shore, 2008

The Pipeline Arena

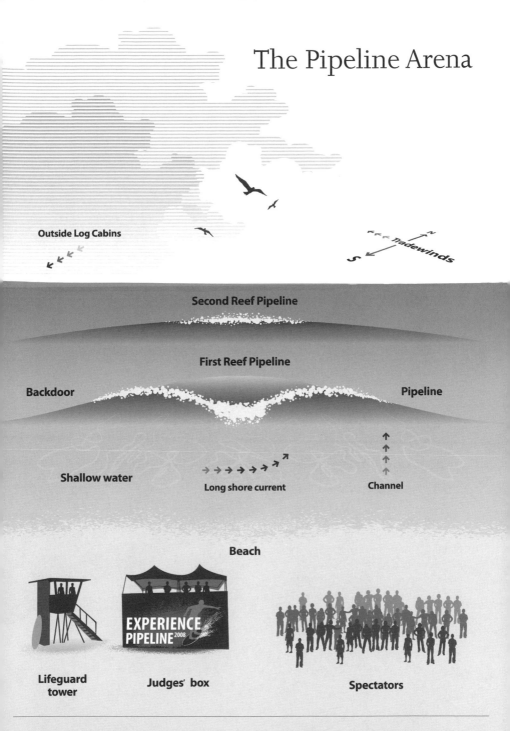

Map of the Pipe Masters contest area. Banzai Pipeline, North Shore, Oahu, Hawaii, USA.
Illustration by Ryan Mcfarlane and Blake Haber.

The Surf at Pipeline

The right-hand wave
breaking off the peak at
Pipeline is called Backdoor.
Backdoor can throw perfect,
hollow tubes, but it can also break
in dangerously unpredictable ways.
It has been known to suck the reef dry,
exposing coral heads that deliver career-
ending injuries to professional surfers.

Cross Section Illustration of Banzai Pipeline, North Shore, Oahu. Artist: Phil Roberts.

Bull and tiger
sharks regularly
patrol the breaks of the
North Shore, and surfers
are sometimes attacked.

The left-hand wave is known
as Pipeline, and it pumps out
perfectly cylindrical barrels.
The narrow channel (which the
arrow points to) contains slightly
deeper water than the rest of the reef
and marks the spot where most waves stop
breaking. The channel is also the best place
for surfers to paddle out to the lineup.

The lip of the wave is thick and fast-falling. Surfers hope to make
it down the wave and into the tube. Below the surface, a seabed of
jagged coral heads and sharp spikes awaits those who wipe out.

How To Read This Book

Grab a coin and start off by reading page 1. At the bottom of the page you will notice the "Flip a coin" icon.

Flip your coin and, based on how it lands (heads or tails), follow the prompt to the page and section indicated. Read only your indicated section, then toss your coin again and follow the prompt on where to go next, and so on, until you reach your ultimate fate at Pipeline. It's as simple as that!

This book has been carefully designed to give you an experience that is as random and full of suspense as surfing Pipeline itself. You can read this book in many different ways: alone, with a quarter by your side; in a group with others—one person flips the coin, another reads the story aloud, everyone enjoys; or you can get creative and turn the book into a party game—make up your own rules and go for it.

Whatever you do, be true to your toss!

Let The Contest Begin!

You, surfer, are on the beach at Pipeline, watching the sets closely as you wait for your heat to begin. The waves thunder across the nearshore reef, forming cavernous blue barrels and explosions of whitewater before rushing up the sand and expiring at your feet. Your pulse races as you focus in on winning the biggest surf contest of the year.

You are about to compete in the Pipe Masters event, the final stop on the professional surfing tour. The battle for the title of world champion has come down to three surfers: local talent Jacala Boy Bones, six-time world champ Neil "Nelly" Yater, and you. The three of you have made it to the final heat, which will begin any moment. The next twenty minutes will determine who wins the World Title of Surfing.

Now you're given the go-ahead to paddle out. There's a lull, so you and your two competitors race for the outside and make it to the lineup without incident. Two large sets roll by before the air horn sounds the official start of the heat.

You look over at Nelly, who nods and says, "This is it, time to go big."

You look at Jacala Boy, who warns with a chuckle: "Eh surfahs! My beach, my waves!"

Just then, a set rises up over Third Reef, some two hundred yards outside. The three of you watch it march in and decide to let the first wave pass, but the second one looks perfect. You out-jockey Nelly, but not Jacala Boy. He's a little deeper than you, but it doesn't look like he's committed himself yet. Nelly, however, looks intent on going, and you are also intent on going. You swing around and start paddling. You're drawn backwards up the wave face, and when you reach the crest you have enough forward momentum to take the drop . . .

Heads - Page 2a   **Flip a coin**   **Tails - Page 4a**

a)

You hear a loud voice to your right warn: "Eh brah! Comin' down!"

It's Jacala Boy Bones, dropping in behind you. The wave is going vertical as you watch him spring to his feet and aim down the face. The wind blows harder offshore, but as the lip propels you forward, you may be irrevocably committed . . .

2

You decide to give this one to Nelly. You watch him paddle hard past you then swing into an awesome wave. The last thing you see is him bottom turning into a fantastic blue bowl. You feel a bit of regret for letting him go, but quickly look out the back for another, hopefully better wave.

b)

a)

It's too late now—you're going too fast. You crash into Jacala Boy Bones and both of you go down hard. Seconds later, Pipeline's guillotine-like lip falls, driving you perilously close to the reef and twisting your limbs every which way in the horrendous washing machine. The spectators on the beach gasp at your blunder and the lifeguards grasp their flotation devices, ready to dive in for a serious heavy-water rescue.

3

Nelly Yater rockets down in front of you, just missing you. You pull into the barrel and it opens wide. You feel like someone's behind you. You look back and see Nelly. He's pumping hard to catch up with you and make it out of the barrel. You know that if he makes it, he might score higher than you for riding so deep in the tube. You actually ponder sabotaging him—after all, he almost slammed into you when he tried to snake you.

b)

a)

Jacala Boy backs out, knowing there are bigger waves to come. At that point you fully commit. The wave, about twenty foot on the face, is seriously starting to jack. You practically freefall into the pit, but make the drop. You look up and see Nelly about to drop in on you. Just before you crank your bottom turn, you whistle sharply up to him.

But now you must focus all your attention on the bowl taking shape before you, or you might get axed by the formidable Pipeline lip.

4

As you watch Jacala Boy exit the tube and kick out, you race for the quickly closing exit, but too late . . . The exit gets cut off by a sharply falling lip, then the entire barrel collapses into itself, imploding like an eggshell shattering—with you caught inside it.

Your body gets wrenched around like a rag doll as the wave keeps spinning and exploding shoreward. You bounce off the reef and feel it rip at your leg, but only when you finally surface can you take stock of any injuries . . .

b)

a)

It's too late to pull back without getting sucked over the falls. You spring to your feet and drive down the wave face at rocket speed, right towards Jacala Boy Bones. Nelly pulls back, exiting the wave. But Jacala Boy is in the middle of his bottom turn, watching you with an infuriated look as your collision course now seems unavoidable. Your only option is to jump off your board, but you could injure yourself seriously doing that.

5

You decide to not worry about Nelly and focus on the exit in front of you instead. You pump a few times for speed and glide out of the wide watery cave. The tube spits a powerful mist at your back, almost blowing you off your board. You look back to see Nelly still riding—he makes it out of the barrel.

You both kick out of the wave and scan the large scoreboard above the judges' box, waiting for your scores. Within twenty seconds the numbers come up, and you're both surprised at the outcome . . .

b)

a)

This wave looks too good to give away during a competition, even if it's Nelly Yater who wants it. You paddle hard and are able to stay ahead of him and get in deeper. As the wave jacks, he pulls back and you hop to your feet and begin aiming down the face. The bottom is dropping out quicker than you anticipated, and you are almost freefalling into the pit.

6

Finally you emerge in a frothy, bubbling cauldron of whitewater. Fortunately, the next wave that breaks is peaking further to the west and inside of you, sparing you a further hammering. As the turbulent water sizzles clearer, Jacala Boy Bones pops up right beside you, holding his shoulder, cursing and moaning. You notice the water around him swirl with red and realize what must have happened: he hit the reef, hard.

You hesitate for a moment, unsure if you should help him or paddle back out and leave his rescue to the water patrol. The way he is cussing, it is clear much of his anger is directed at you. Will he even allow you to help him without pouncing on you for causing him to wipe out?

For a few seconds you ponder the best course of action, then decide . . .

b)

a)

Fortunately, at the last second Nelly pulls back. A huge barrel takes shape around you and the lip falls like a heavy waterfall clean to your side. The cavern is turquoise in color and crystal clear, and you see a photographer filming you as you stand up proudly inside the impressive tube. After riding in the barrel for what seems like an eternity, you see its end starting to close. You jam to make it through the closing gap. If you blow it now, your perfect tube ride will garner only meager points. You're driving at full speed as the entire cavern begins to cave in.

7

Before you can think about it for another second, you scream by Jacala Boy, missing him by inches, then crank a bottom turn and just squeak under the lip as you pull into the barrel behind him. You watch in amazement as you both ride through the expansive blue room. You are so deep that you can feel a strange suction of air around you, popping your eardrums as if you were descending in an airplane. There's a great rumble as an avalanche of whitewater snowballs at your back. You see Jacala Boy exit the barrel, so you begin pumping for more speed in hopes of making it out before the tube implodes on you.

b)

a)

Nelly is fast on your tail when you decide to sabotage him. You slow down just enough for him to ride up beside you, then reach out and push his face, causing him to fall off his board and get worked in the pit.

Now that the six-time world champ is down, you refocus on the barrel exit and just squeak out in time before the entire cavern collapses, shooting forth a powerful, spitting wind. You throw your arms up in victory so that the judges and spectators will clearly see you've made the tube, then you launch off the back of the wave, kicking out.

8

You have good fortune, or perhaps it's instinct: a beautiful wave is rising before you, better than any you've seen all day.

You paddle to get deeper, then pivot around and stroke hard to get into it. You drop down the face while digging your arm into the wave. The lip falls, and you stand tall and proud in a gaping barrel, the roaring vortex cascading around you. You blast out through a hole of sunshine. A rush of wind and wave spit pushes at your back.

You slowly ride off the back of the wave, throwing your arms up in glory as the pit roars to a close beneath you. Not long after, you look shoreward to see a series of solid scores, and one of them is a 10!

b)

a)

Suddenly you feel the reef tear into your thigh and see the water around you swirl red. You hold your leg and struggle upwards, surfacing beside Jacala Boy Bones as you both gasp for air. He looks at you with fierce anger, then turns and dives under the water again. You look up and see why: another set wave is about to unload on you. You take a quick breath and duck under the surface . . . but not in time. The wave crashes into you, knocking you silly. Fortunately, you don't hit the reef a second time.

When you resurface, Jacala Boy is swimming towards you, cussing angrily like he is going to pounce on you.

You hold a hand up and cry, "Sorry, Jacala Boy! There was nothing I could do! I hit the reef and my leg's pretty jacked!"

9

You grab the rails of your board and pull hard back from the cresting breaker. You teeter at the wave's ledge for a terrifying moment, about to get sucked over the falls! But the breaker lets you off—you go floating over its back without incident. You breathe a sigh of relief and see Nelly pull back as well. The last you see of Jacala Boy Bones is him about to pull into the barrel.

"Wow, JB got a nice one!" Nelly calls to you. "Our turn next!"

Another set wave is rising before you. Nelly starts paddling hard, trying to get better positioning than you. His competitive spirit is strong. You consider letting him have his way with this one, hoping there'll be a better wave behind it. But as the roller begins to peak up, you realize it's going to be a big, fantastic wave with a smooth and sane drop. Nelly is just about level with you when you make your decision . . .

b)

a)

You try to keep the nose of your board from gouging the trough as the wave sucks out and becomes radically concave. You can see the tube already taking form above you as you negotiate the drop. Even if you make it to the bottom, you will have to gun it with all you've got just to outrun the lip.

Your anxieties climax as you see the nose of your board beginning to pearl. You hope it won't drive deeper, but it does: the entire front half of your board thrusts underwater, sending you diving into the trough. Your body is whipped face-first into the water.

10

Just when you think you've cleared the lip and made it out of the barrel, you feel the lip slam into your head, knocking you down. You emerge behind the wave in flat water. You watch the back of the wave as it rolls steadily shoreward. You tug at your leash, drawing your board to you, then sit up and glance towards the beach. The scores have already been tallied. You see nothing above a five. A perfect 10 might have been there had you only made it! Fuming, you paddle back to the lineup and wait for another set.

b)

a)

You pump your board as fast as you can, just squeaking out of the barrel as it slams shut behind you with a ferocious explosion of whitewater and spit. A second tube section takes form in front of you. You react instinctively by pulling in. The second tube section has beautiful form. You ride it with perfect poise, then kick out the back.

You are interested to see how you scored. Will you be rewarded for riding deep and long through the two barrel sections, or will riding behind Jacala Boy be deemed interference, thereby reducing your ride's overall score?

11

You wait for many long minutes, for as long as it takes Nelly to paddle back out. But, to your dismay, there's a lull and you don't catch anything in the interim. Worse, you look back at Nelly's score to see all high points. You realize that it will require a far more aggressive approach on your part if you are to get the edge on Nelly.

"Nice ride, Neil," you tell him for good sportsmanship, but inside you are fuming.

"Thanks," he says as he paddles right past you, taking position further outside. You worry that if a bomb comes, he'll catch it.

Jacala Boy Bones is sitting deeper than you, more towards Backdoor. Your competitors have taken strategic positions in the lineup, and this makes you concerned.

b)

a)

You look back and see all high scores raised for you—the judges and the audience did not see your dirty deed behind the curtain of water as you rode in the tube with Nelly. You're stoked to start your heat off with a high-scoring wave. You paddle back to the outside and wait with Jacala Boy Bones for another wave.

A few minutes pass without another set. You don't even notice that Nelly has paddled up beside you until he splashes you with water and yells: "You fouling kook! That was interference!"

"All's fair in war, champ," you respond coolly, never taking your eyes off the horizon.

12

Your leg is messed up. It is throbbing with pain and bleeding steadily. Jacala Boy paddles over and looks at you sternly.

"Ho cuz, you alright oh wot?" he says.

"Jacala Boy—it's my leg. I'm telling you, I think it could be serious."

"Eh, let me look, brah," he answers without emotion.

You slide off the side of your board and attempt to lift your leg out of the water. By now, both of you aren't so sure you want to see how bad it really is.

b)

a)

You emerge from the barrel into the bright afternoon sunshine. You can hear the crowd on the beach erupt in cheers as the powerful bowl implodes behind you, sending forth a rocketing wind. You throw your arms up like a winning prizefighter and emit a great howl. You glide over the top of the wave, escaping successfully over the back. Your pulse is racing from both a spectacular barrel and the chance of scoring high. You scan the judges' box on the beach and the large numbers soon show over them.

Your scores are all high, with one a 9.7—near perfect.

"Yeah!" you exclaim, then put your nose down and begin paddling back towards the lineup. It's a good start, but far too soon to get comfortable. You take your position in the lineup and wait for another set.

13

To the amazement of the spectators, you make the insanely steep drop, but you're thrown off balance for a moment. You regain your footing and crank a hard bottom turn as you watch the lip pitching out. The tube is starting to freight-train. You struggle to angle up towards the face and get clear of the guillotine-like lip. You see it falling directly over you and try to duck beneath it into the barrel.

b)

a)

You remember that you're in a contest, where there's no time to lose, so you decide not to help Jacala Boy. After all, that's what the water patrol is for. You begin paddling away from him.

"Ay brah, where you goin' all wiki wiki?!" he cries out to you. "My shoulda all chewed up! Won't you help me, brah?"

"Help's on the way," you yell back as the water rescue team enters the water. "I'm going to try and catch a few more waves."

"I'm gonna get you, brah!" JB yells as he paddles towards you. "You no help Jacala Boy, you go down too!"

He can't paddle well with his injury, so you keep a good distance ahead of him. The water patrol are gaining on him.

14

Your scores are tied exactly!

"Unbelievable!" Nelly exclaims, shaking his head.

"I'm not going to give you the edge so easy," you reply in jest.

Nelly ignores you and begins stroking further outside.

Jacala Boy Bones is sitting about twenty yards to your west. He always seems to find the deepest positioning, even if that means he takes a beating for it now and then. He makes eye contact with you, so you nod in a comradely way. He shakes his head in the negative.

The intensity is heating up. It looks like they want the win maybe more that you do.

b)

a)

A massive wall grows off of Third Reef—a rogue wave that makes you wonder if you've paddled out with a big enough board. You and your competitors stroke hard seaward, believing it will break at Second Reef.

At first Jacala Boy seems to have the best positioning, being the furthest out and paddling the hardest towards the great roller. As the wave rises over Second Reef, he spins around and starts stroking hard to catch it, but the wave momentarily holds back and does not let him on. Seconds later, the wave is bouncing to life, jacking ever higher before you and Nelly.

"It's mine!" Nelly cries, his arms in full blender mode as he tries to muscle his way over the ledge.

"Not so fast, champ!" you shout back, stroking hard just beside him—and in better position.

15

You turn to see your score, having a good feeling that it will be high. To your dismay, the judges are all holding up the letter D—which means your ride was disqualified. They saw your intentional interference with Nelly, so you get no points for all that effort.

You paddle back out to the lineup, cursing left and right.

Nelly makes it back outside quicker than you would have liked. He starts telling you off, but you just ignore him.

b)

a)

Your Bermuda trunks are torn across the side of your thigh, but you're relieved to see no signs of bodily injury. There is no blood, no scrapes or cuts on your leg.

"Phew!" you say, exhaling heavily. "That was a close one!"

You look shoreward and the scores go up. Most are quite low, of course, but a 6.5 helps to redeem your bruised ego. Still, you know you'll have to do better. You lie on your board and paddle back outside, focusing more than ever on this contest.

16

You take a serious beating underwater. Jagged coral tickles your scalp. You finally surface, fortunate that you have not hit the reef hard. You tug on your leash, drawing your board to you. It's still in one piece.

Your equilibrium is slightly out of whack from slamming your eardrum when you hit the wave's trough. You lie over your board and tilt your head sideways. Water drips from your ear. Your equilibrium normalizes. You shimmy all the way onto your board and begin paddling back out.

Suddenly a fifteen-foot wave walls up in front of you! The blood freezes in your veins. You stroke for your life towards the rapidly jacking wall. It throws a heavy lip down at you at full speed. You extend your body and board to the limit, watching the lip come down. Will you make the duck-dive or get caught inside?

b)

a)

Nelly's ride was disqualified for interference, while you scored fairly high. He splashes the water in frustration, then begins paddling back out towards the lineup.

"Hey, no worries, Nelly," you comment, then begin stroking just behind him.

You see him shake his head, totally aggravated. His tube ride, after all, was far deeper. If you hadn't had been on that wave, his scores would have been impressive.

"There'll be more waves, brah," you say, trying to ease some of the tension. Nelly just paddles faster.

17

The scores come up and you and Jacala Boy are both amazed. While your ride was far more spectacular, you scored low due to your interference.

"You should be disqualified from da heat, brah!" Jacala Boy chides you.

"What's the matter, JB?" you shout back. "Can't hotdog a meaty section?"

"Eh brah? Wat you say? Like beef, brah?"

"Beef?" you ask. "No thanks, I'm a vegetarian."

You decide not to distract yourself messing with Jacala Boy, so you paddle back outside and wait for another set.

b)

a)

Back out in the lineup, waiting for another set, you see a large shadow pass over, or beneath the water. You look up towards the sun, thinking perhaps a plane has just passed overhead, but to your alarm, the sky is clear.

Just then, a large dorsal fin juts out of the water and begins circling the three of you in a wide, elliptical pattern. A huge tiger shark has entered the lineup and is closing in. Its revolutions grow tighter and tighter as it moves in for a likely attack. You and your competitors do your best to raise your legs out of the water. To paddle would be foolish—it would only encourage it to go after the splashing one.

There are no waves on the horizon and the shark is beginning to make erratic maneuvers, darting between the three of you and bumping your boards. Your eyes go wide when you get a good look at the shark: it is sixteen feet long, with the girth of a small car.

18

You decide to help Jacala Boy and begin paddling slowly towards him. He looks at you with great anxiety, then at his shoulder. It's chewed up pretty bad.

"I'll be alright, brah," he says stoically, but there's no masking the worried tone in his voice.

"Let's have a look at that shoulder, Jacala Boy," you say as you maneuver towards him.

"Come closer, brah," he says, his voice and expression on edge.

You stop in front of him, and he firmly grabs the nose of your board.

b)

a)

Jacala Boy continues paddling towards you, ranting all the while. You easily outpaddle him.

The water patrol are quick to make it through the channel and out to him. His white jersey has turned blood-red.

Jacala Boy tries to push them aside, still trying to get to you and shouting: "Nobody mess wid Jacala Boy! It's not ova between us!"

The water patrol ultimately calm him down and help him back to shore. You sit up on your board and see another set approaching.

19

You float on your back and raise your leg out of the water. There are deep gashes, which bleed steadily.

"Punk!" Jacala Boy curses at you. "You one dum banana!"

"But Jacala Boy!" you plead. "My leg!"

He approaches you angrily, grabs your board and pushes it towards the beach. The leash tugs on your leg, causing sharp pain.

"Time for you to get out, brah!" he taunts, then laughs boorishly and paddles far outside.

Rollers pass under you as you retrieve your board and paddle further into the channel. You sit up and study your leg more closely while trying to keep your balance.

b)

a)

"Is that what you call good sportsmanship?!" Nelly continues. "I ought to knock your lights out!"

"Then you'd better make it quick, or the judges will see it," you chide back, extending your jaw and pointing to it.

Nelly glances back at the judges' box on the beach. In between sets, it's obvious they have a clear view of the lineup. He hedges, then lowers his fist and splashes you instead.

"Pipe down, champ," you laugh. "You've won the world title six times. If you want to win it again, you're going to have to outsurf me."

"Shouldn't be hard," he replies coolly.

He paddles further out. You follow him with quiet paddle strokes.

20

You just make it under the lip and into a humongous barrel. The crowds lining the beach hold their breath in utter suspense. The blue cylinder is perfectly round and the lip falls beside you like a heavy waterfall. You hear a loud suction noise and see whitewater snowballing at you from deep within the tube. You pump a few times for more speed, then emerge into sunlight to explosive cheers from the spectators. But as far as you're concerned, your ride has just begun!

There's still a tall, clean wall next to you, and it's going vertical again. You crank a hard bottom turn, aiming towards the midday sun. The crowd is cheering as you rocket straight up into an off-the-lip on this triple-overhead wave. Will you be counted amongst Pipeline surfing legends for sticking a move like this? You snap off the lip and feel yourself going weightless when it starts to pitch. You trust to providence as you rock your full weight to your back leg, trying to land the move.

b)

a)

After interminable minutes of waiting, a set finally comes. It's not a clean series of waves; the walls are irregular and shifty. Nelly manages to pick off a big mushburger that breaks early. He carves up the face before streaking down into the First Reef pit. The wave doesn't tube all that well, forcing him to ride ahead of the break for most of the high-points barrel section. He kicks out a short time later and you watch for his score. His points are in the 5 to 7 range—quite weak, really.

Suddenly, a good wave peaks up before you and Jacala Boy. You both look to go left, but the crest it is already crumbling down.

You and Jacala Boy look right and see a nice Backdoor section forming. You paddle hard to maneuver deeper than Jacala Boy, but he shows no sign of backing off. You let out a sharp whistle, but he ignores you. A split second later the wave sucks up vertically and you spring to your feet.

21

You've outjockeyed your opponents, and you have a skyscraping Second Reef wave all to yourself. This is your chance to score big! You muscle your way over the ledge as the wave starts bouncing at the lip and aim down the face. You're making a spectacular drop when you realize the wave is sucking dry! The water below is only a foot or two deep. You're terrified that the water will suck completely off the reef. If it does, you will be in a world of pain.

You hesitate. Should you bail out while you can still control your dive? Or should you stick to your line? You can't decide what to do . . .

b)

a)

You get pounded so fiercely underwater that you don't know which way is up. You can't hold your breath much longer. You try to remain calm, but when you struggle for the surface and knock a fist into the reef, you get freaked out.

Well, at least now I know which way is up, you think, then spin around and launch off the reef.

Seconds later, you break the surface and the world looks as if it's been tilted sideways. You've blown an eardrum.

"Damn it!" you curse. You find your board and paddle towards the channel. You're pissed off. You don't even care what you scored on that wave.

In the safety of the channel, you sit up on your board to assess the situation. Is there any way you can keep competing, or is the contest over for you?

22

Jacala Boy paddles in a mad rage and quickly gains on you.

"Haole no help local boy in need?" he screams. "Leave Oahu now!"

"Wait, Jacala Boy!" you cry as he pulls at your leash. Hoping to avoid his fists, you undo your leash and push your board at him, then backstroke away. He sits up on his board and lifts yours out of the water.

"A tri-fin, brah!" he taunts. He puts a big hand on the right fin. Crraack! Then the left fin. Crraack!

"Ah ha ha!" he laughs as he tosses your board back to you. "Now you ride single fin, brah! Welcome to da fifties all ova!"

b)

a)

The scores are raised and you are stoked! Your points are much higher than Jacala Boy's, with one being a 9.5!

"That's right, JB!" you call over to him, taunting him, then you paddle further outside.

He seems to follow you, but you aren't paying too much attention to him. It's more important for you to focus on the horizon and try to pick off another high-scoring wave.

23

You and your rivals settle into your positions in the lineup. You're pondering getting better positioning when suddenly you are startled out of your wits.

A large sea-turtle, six feet in length, surfaces next to you. It looks up at you curiously; its bent, beak-like nose and beady eyes give it a mesmerizing appearance.

"It's mating season, brah!" Jacala Boy teases.

Just then a set rises forth, swinging towards Backdoor. You begin paddling for better positioning, but the turtle is right in your way!

"Move!" you yell at it. You paddle left, then right. Somehow the turtle remains in front. It seems to swim wherever you try to paddle, blocking your access. You can hear Nelly and Jacala Boy laughing as they get better positioning.

b)

a)

The lip comes down on you like a load of bricks, landing squarely on your shoulders, tweaking your neck, and driving you into the depths.

Eventually you pop up out of the water and pull on your leash. Your board is still intact. You're worried about your neck, so you paddle beyond the breakers, then sit up on your board and flex your neck to test it out. It feels sore, but not seriously injured. You are still in the competition.

"What happened?" Nelly calls over. "Did you get axed?"

You just shrug your shoulders. It's none of his business, really, and you refuse to concede one ounce of defeat until the final scores are tallied. As for your score on this ride, you don't even bother looking. Now that you've weathered a good beating, you've built confidence to charge harder.

24

Jacala Boy pushes your board away and says: "You bring evil to da Pipe. Go back to da mainland!"

"But Jacala Boy," you plead, "I'm only trying to help."

"Wat brah? How's that? How can you help me now? No, brah, I don't think so. Jacala Boy take care of himself! In Hawaii, we don't need folks like you to come and play king for a day. I may be spillin' blood, brah, but it only make me more determined! Now get away!"

He groans momentarily as he covers his wound with his hand.

You are perplexed, but you do as he requests. Slowly you paddle further outside, leaving the injured and bleeding Jacala Boy to his own whims and devices.

b)

a)

Suddenly, the shark thrashes around and bites into your leg! You scream in pain, then punch at its head to no avail.

The water turns blood red, and you watch in horror as the shark thrashes from side, gnawing deeper into your muscle. It rolls a bit and looks up at you with a sinister black eyeball. You feel like you are looking into the eye of death! Then you remember what you read in a book about how to ward off a shark attack— you gouge your finger into its eye.

It immediately backs off and submerges out of sight.

"Oooow, my leg!" you moan.

25

You and Jacala Boy drop in at the same time. Everything is happening extremely fast—it's literally a blur. The rail of his board hits yours, throwing you both off balance. The wave's lip pitches out over the shallow reef.

b)

a)

The wave sucks dry to your left. Without a moment's hesitation, you go right. As you bottom turn, a huge Backdoor section pitches out. The spectators on the beach all get to their feet as you pull under the lip.

26

Nelly reaches over and socks you in the ear. Instantly there's a loud ringing sound, and your ear throbs with pain.

"That's what you get for being a punk!" he admonishes.

You look back towards the beach to see if the judges saw the incident, but there are no red flags raised.

"That was really low, bro," you say.

"All's fair in war—and contests!" he replies with a sneer.

Your equilibrium is slightly out of whack. You fear he may have blown out one of your eardrums.

"Do what you have to do to win, Nelly," you say in a biting tone. You paddle to the channel and sit up on your board to regain your bearings.

b)

a)

The lip explodes into you, knocking you silly. Pipeline lips are said to hit like a sledgehammer, and you're feeling the full force of that description.

But you are lucky—you don't hit the reef. Somehow, in the maelstrom of churning whitewater, you're lifted up to the surface. You feel shaken by the onslaught but are unharmed.

You notice there isn't the slightest tug of your leash at your ankle. Did your leash snap? Or worse, did your board break?

You reach down and grab the leash at your ankle, giving it a firm tug. You search the foamy surface for signs of your stick and are amazed at what you see . . .

27

You raise your leg out of the water. It's torn open badly.

"Shoot, brah," Jacala says, flinching, "we betta get you in."

On the beach, the water patrol are running a Jet Ski into the water.

"Jacala Boy," you ask, "will you call the water patrol off? I want to finish this debacle unassisted. I can get in alright on my own."

He lets out a sharp whistle, then waves the water patrol back.
He gives you a push towards the channel and says, "Aloha, brah."

You paddle in, then limp stoically up the beach.

b)

a)

You fall sideways, slamming into the wave's trough. You see the massive barrel cascade over you and watch Jacala Boy regain his balance and pull in before you submerge underwater.

A terrifying feeling spreads through you as you feel the powerful wave begin to suck you back up towards the lip. If you go over the falls on this Backdoor beast, you could easily die.

28

Suddenly the shark lunges out of the water towards Jacala Boy.

"Jacala!" you yell as you see its jaws clamp onto his shoulder, taking him down.

Jacala Boy resurfaces, holding on to the shark's dorsal fin and punching its head with solid blows. The two of them go under again.

A long time passes. You can't see anything beneath you. Then Jacala Boy breaks the surface and swims back to his board. The shark is nowhere in sight. Jacala climbs onto his board, then puts his hand over his injured shoulder and groans.

You begin paddling towards him, but hesitate for a moment. Do you really want to get involved? Helping him may lose you the contest. Now that he's out of the picture, you only have Nelly to contend with.

b)

a)

Suddenly you see the shark's dorsal fin pop up right next to you.

"Jacala! Help!" you scream.

The noble Hawaiian surfer looks over at you as the shark bites into your bleeding leg again. It pulls you off your board, gnaws through your leash, then drags you down into the depths. Bubbles escape from your mouth and mix with the cauldron of bloody water.

You catch a glimpse of your board floating some twenty feet above and see Jacala Boy paddling over to it. The shark is shaking you around underwater like a rag doll, and you're almost out of breath.

You make a last, desperate attempt to ward it off by socking its nose with a series of quick, powerful jabs. It thrashes you around violently, but you keep up your counterattack.

29

You feel well enough to continue competing.

Phew! you think. That could have cost me the contest!

You settle into position in the lineup, trying to shake off some lingering pain.

b)

a)

You race down the face and just as you initiate your bottom turn, Jacala Boy rockets down in front of you, missing you by inches.

You're frustrated about being snaked. You try to focus on the wave, but as the lip throws, you glance behind you and see Jacala Boy trying to bottom turn under the falling lip.

30

The water patrol reach you moments later, pulling you back to the surface. The water around you is red, and your face is turning blue. They rush you to shore and lay you on a backboard.

"Okay, ready?" one of them calls out. "Pump – one – two – three!"

They begin giving you CPR, pressing on your chest and breathing into your mouth. They feel for your pulse, listen for your breath.

"Still nothing," one of them says, and they resume CPR.

After twenty minutes of intensive effort, the water patrol cover your body with a towel and bow their heads.

"Ladies and gentlemen," a correspondent speaks into his microphone before a row of cameras, "a finalist has drowned while competing in the Pipe Masters event."

The End

a)

Jacala Boy pulls you to him.

"Oow, ooow," he moans. "My shoulda really messed up."

"Okay, Jacala Boy," you say consolingly, "we're gonna get you in. Just lie on your board and grab my leash with your good arm. I'll do all the paddling."

He does as you say. You wait for a lull, then began stroking hard shoreward. It's difficult towing the big Hawaiian, but you gain momentum and get past the impact zone to the inside. The water patrol lift him from the shallows and onto the beach.

The spectators applaud the rescue, but you humbly ignore the fanfare and paddle back out to finish your heat.

31

Your collision with Jacala Boy causes him to fall. You see him tumbling over the water behind you just before you pull into a gaping barrel. You feel both happiness and remorse: you are glad Jacala Boy went down rather than you, but you regret that he will take a heavy beating over Backdoor's shallow reef.

Now you must make this barrel, or your fate will be no different than JB's . . .

b)

a)

Your leg is slightly injured, but it's not as bad as you originally feared. There are a few gouges, but no main veins appear to have been cut. You move your limb around to test its mobility, then poke at the lacerations. The pain is manageable and your leg still feels flexible and strong.

You look towards the beach and see the water patrol jumping into action. You emit a sharp whistle then point shoreward, indicating they should turn back, which they do. You pull off your lycra jersey and tie it tightly around the worst part of your chewed-up leg. This almost completely stops your blood from escaping, without cutting off circulation.

"I'm not through yet!" you shout to your opponents.

They look back at you showing no emotion. You paddle back towards the lineup, ready to take on anything that moves!

32

When the first wave comes, you and Nelly try to outmaneuver one another. When you notice how small the wave is, you back off. Nelly backs off as well. Set waves tend to grow in succession, and your heart starts pounding when you see the next one coming. It's much further out—so far, in fact, that you and Nelly will both get caught inside.

"Damn!" says Nelly as he paddles madly towards the channel. "I should've followed my instincts and gone for that first one!"

Me too, you think, as you both get caught directly in the path of a watery avalanche!

b)

a)

You wait for another wave, fondly recalling your previous ride and the high score you achieved. Suddenly, out of nowhere, Jacala Boy lands his fist on your jaw.

"Hey!" you shout, spitting blood. "What the f—"

"Ay, brah!" he taunts. "Welcome to Hawaii!"

A dark set looms over the outer reefs. You start paddling west to get away from Jacala Boy.

With a little luck, you think, I'll take off deep on the first set wave and evade JB.

33

You wait a few more minutes, but things don't improve. The horizon is still tilted, your hearing is still off, and you become increasingly nauseous. You realize there's no way you'll be able to surf Pipe in this condition.

You look out towards the lineup and see Nelly bobbing there in his bright jersey. You grow furious looking at him. I can't let him win, you think.

Suddenly, you see a set rising over the outer reefs. You watch Nelly spring into action. Without wasting another second, you stroke hard towards him— anything to keep him from catching another wave!

Nelly passes on the first wave. You're almost to him when the second wave comes. He turns and paddles for it. You reach for his leash as inconspicuously as you can . . .

b)

a)

You watch in frustration as both Jacala Boy and Nelly get nice waves while the turtle still blocks your access. Finally you manage to stroke around it.

The third wave of the set barrels big before your eyes, completely unridden. "There goes my winning wave, reptile!" you say to the turtle.

To your relief there's a fourth wave, and it looks just as good as the previous one. You pivot around and paddle with all your might to get into it. Faster and faster the water sucks off the reef below as the thick Pipeline comber lunges shoreward. You spring to your feet and aim vertically down the steeply concaving wall. To your horror you realize the wave might actually suck dry and drive you directly into the sharp and craggy reef!

34

The nose of your board pearls. You force your weight over the tail and the nose pops back out of the water, preventing your whole board from pearling. You reach the trough, then crank a bottom turn and set up for another round barrel section, which you make with ease. You fling yourself off the back of the wave and raise your clenched fists in victory as the crowd erupts in rapturous cheering and applause.

You paddle slowly back out, looking all the while towards shore to watch for your scores: 9.7, 9.5, 9.3, and 9.9!

"Yes!" you shout. You stroke further outside and sit up on your board. Your opponents see your confident expression and know they may be in a bit of trouble.

b)

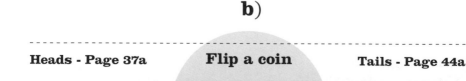

Heads - Page 147a   **Flip a coin**   **Tails - Page 153b**

a)

Your equilibrium is so off-kilter that there's no way you can continue surfing. You paddle to shore, head lowered in resignation.

On the beach, the medics assist you under the shade of the judges' box. You look out at the surf. Your rival pulls into a big barrel and makes it out. The crowd erupts in cheers.

You kick the sand and slap your thigh in anger.

As medics drain water from your ears, a man approaches. You don't recognize him at first. You look at his face and then you remember. The reason you didn't recognize him is because he is dressed in business casual: collared shirt, khaki pants, and blazer.

35

He tosses your board—now a single-fin—back at you.

"Now, brah," he sneers, a murderous expression crossing his brows, "Jacala Boy gonna smash off yo ears!"

You scramble onto your board and begin stroking away from him in terror.

Just then, a water patrolman seizes JB from behind and says: "We have determined you are unfit to continue in the competition. We're taking you in for medical attention."

"What?!" Jacala Boy quips. "Pipe is a gladiator pit, everybody bleed here! Eh! You take me in? How's that?"

Jacala Boy continues his protests, but soon gives in and is taken to shore.

b)

Heads - Page 48b   **Flip a coin**   **Tails - Page 57a**

a)

The wave detonates ferociously behind you as you push through your duck-dive. You resurface out the back and take a deep breath of air.

Another large wave crests before your eyes, but you make it under this one with a bit more room to spare. You resurface, concerned there will be a bigger one yet—but there isn't.

"Phew!" you exclaim, shaking your head from side to side in disbelief. You resume your position in the lineup, draining water from your nose and ears and catching your breath as you wait for another set.

36

You hold your line and bottom turn going left. It's so shallow that you fear your skegs will catch the reef. But you rise out of the bottom turn without incident and into a speedy tube.

Suddenly a coral head pops up out of the water directly in front of you. There's no way you can turn around it without getting drilled by the lip and you can't take a higher line around it. You're left with only one option: to try and pull an air over the coral head.

You set your feet in ollie formation and pop clean out of the water just before you hit the ugly, exposed clump. You look down and see the coral head passing beneath your board—but that same old dread comes to you again: Will your skegs hit it, destroying your board and you in the process? Or will you clear this dangerous obstacle deep within the barrel?

b)

a)

It isn't long before another set starts to hit.

"Just clear out!" Jacala Boy exclaims, as you all jockey for the first wave.

"No way, not this time!" Nelly ripostes, as he tries to get the edge.

You're paddling hard, sprinting for the peak beside your opponents, and the three of you are practically on top of each other as the wave gets ready to break. You all get to your feet and aim down the face. You can't help thinking of surfing in the 1950s, when everyone would go on the same wave with no regard for safety or rank.

37

Your leg is in worse shape than you thought. There are deep lacerations, which have begun to bleed profusely. You aim towards shore and begin paddling in, but soon become faint. You see the water patrol on the sand and signal them for help. They rush into the water; one swims out to you with a life preserver, another paddles out on a longboard.

A large set explodes behind you, and after the whitewater lopes a few times, it blasts you from behind, knocking you off your board and spinning you around underwater. You lose all sense of direction and struggle for the surface. You get nowhere—you're not even sure which way is up any more. Are you swimming sideways, up, or down? Everything around you is swirling and bubbling blue, white, and red. You start to panic. You're almost completely out of breath. Alas, you give in, opening your mouth and trying to breathe. Your lungs fill with water and everything goes black.

b)

a)

The lip hits Jacala Boy like a heavy hammer, drilling him into the shallows. You feel a tinge of vindication knowing he's getting worked and will come up with low points at best.

You look ahead of you and see a gaping Backdoor barrel encircling you. This is your big chance to pull out a perfect-scoring wave. You gird yourself for whatever the wave may do next.

38

As the tortoise continues to impede your progress, you watch Jacala Boy and Nelly get big rides from the set. Another perfect wave pumps in and the sea-turtle still bars your way. Whenever you try to paddle around it, it swims in your direction, shutting off access. You can feel the contest slipping through your fingers.

Frantically you paddle right up onto the turtle's back. It rises out of the water as you attempt to paddle over it. You have to push yourself off the turtle's back using your feet. Once you clear it, you paddle hard for the lineup.

b)

a)

Just then the water patrol, who had been hastily making their way out to Jacala Boy, seize him from behind.

"Eh!" he yells in protest. "Wot you doin', brah!"

"We're taking you in," a muscular water patrolman retorts as he pins him to a longboard. "Pipeline is no place to surf when you're this thrashed."

"Eh brah!" Jacala says. "I'm from here—I do wot I want!" He resists, but his severely injured shoulder hampers his efforts. They take him back to the beach, and you surreptitiously swap your board for his—a Hawaiian big-wave gun. You paddle it towards the outer reefs.

39

When the first wave comes, both you and Nelly let it pass. You know the first wave of the set is usually the smallest. Furthermore, if you miss it, you run a high risk of getting caught inside by the waves behind it.

The second wave, however, is forming a sweet left. Nelly also recognizes the quality of this one, and a split second later you are trying to outpaddle one another for pole position—or the deepest slot to go left.

As the wave rears up, Nelly tries to squeak by you to claim the wave.

b)

a)

You wake up on a beach with several anxious faces looking down at you. A red-haired medic looks at you and says, "You've pulled through. How do you feel?"

"Not so hot," you say, as she holds your hand.

"What's your name?" she says, testing your brain and memory.

"Look, I know who I am," you answer in irritation. "Just do whatever you need to do and do it quickly—I'm going back out!"

"Sorry, hero," she replies. "The contest is over for you. You're lucky to be alive." She puts an IV in your arm to prepare for a likely transfusion. You're lifted onto a stretcher.

40

To your amazement, Jacala Boy soon joins you out in the lineup. You study his shoulder injury and see that he's applied a swath of surfboard traction pad over the gash. There's a bare spot on the deck of his board from where he pulled it.

"Jacala Boy," you say, "I can't believe that traction pad still sticks after you took it off your board!"

"Yeah, brah," he replies soberly, "it hold to my shoulda okay. I just put it on my stick this morning, so it still planney sticky. But now da deck of my stick is without bumps. Got Sticky Bumps, brah?"

"Actually, I do!" you reply, happy to be of some assistance. You dig into your trunks pocket and toss him a small piece of surf wax.

"Tanks, brah," he says with a kindly wink. "Aloha!"

b)

a)

Your board pops up to the surface in one piece—the wave held it down longer than it held you!

You've been pushed further inside and the water is shallow. As you reach for your board, you step down . . .

41

As Nelly tries to glide into the wave, you find his trailing leash and give it a hard tug, causing him to stop dead and miss the wave.

"Punk!" he curses, then looks in towards the beach with his arms raised, yelling, "Didn't you see that?!"

The scoreboard remains blank—no interference penalty is indicated.

"Punk!" he says again, cocking his fist. But then his eyes widen.

You turn back to see a macking wave rising up behind you. Nelly begins paddling towards you, so you start back-paddling away from him. He comes within striking distance.

"An eye for an eye!" he says angrily, shoving you off your board.

b)

a)

Unfortunately, you're too late. The set is over, and while your rivals got nice rides, you got nothing. Now the sea-turtle swims towards you. It pops its head out of the water and looks at you. You grab it by the neck in a rage.

"Eh brah!" Jacala Boy screams, paddling towards you with great energy and speed. "Do not harm dat green sea-turtle! That's my ohana 'aumakua, my family's animal spirit!"

You listen to his words as you continue to choke the tortoise and stare into the clumsy creature's beady black eyes.

"I'm warning you, brah!" Jacala Boy hollers. "Let go da tortoise now!"

42

Jacala Boy just makes it under the heavy lip behind you. You refocus your attention on what's ahead of you, for you know the barrel at Backdoor can be difficult to make. The tube is turquoise blue and cavernous, and it looks like it will stay open for you.

Suddenly, Jacala Boy rides up beside you.

"Try move, brah!" he yells angrily. "Nobody get in da way of Jacala Boy!" He grabs your jersey and tugs at it fiercely, trying to make you fall.

"Hands off!" you scream, starting to go off-balance.

You both race ahead of the barrel. You try to keep your balance as Jacala Boy continues to tug at your jersey. A second barrel section begins to pitch out . . .

b)

a)

Once you're situated on the outside, you turn to look back at Jacala Boy. He's sitting up, holding his shoulder and swaying from side to side. Suddenly he falls off his board. You paddle over, but before you get to him his board tombstones, indicating that he has sunk.

You find the end of his leash and pull him up hand-over-hand. The weight on the end of the leash is completely motionless.

You get him to the surface, roll him on to his board and perform two quick rescue breaths. No response! You start CPR compressions, and then see a monstrous set approaching. You call out to Nelly for help. You wave to the water patrol. Now the first wave surges and you're not sure if Nelly or the water patrol registered your call.

43

Suddenly you can see the reef only one foot beneath the surface!

Good Lord! you pray, hoping the wave won't suck dry.

You continue to rocket through the barrel as it bowls around you, paranoid that at any second your skegs will hit the reef.

"C'mon baby!" you plead frantically. "Hang in there!"

As you near the barrel exit, you see some unusual boils welling up directly in your path. To your horror, a coral head pops up and your skegs bounce over the reef.

You've heard horror stories of this wave sucking dry in the barrel, and now you're facing that nightmare yourself.

b)

a)

The three of you see a lump on the horizon, then two lumps, then three massive waves rising ominously over the outer reefs. The crests bounce as the large rollers comb the deep reefs. The three of you wait, anticipating the ride of your lives.

You steel yourself for the challenge and paddle deeper than your competitors.

"You're too deep," Nelly warns.

"Maybe, maybe not," you retort smugly as the first wave rises skyward.

44

Jacala Boy keeps pursuing you, even though the first set wave is approaching fast. The wave is bigger and peaking further out than you had anticipated—you and JB are already caught inside. As the crest pitches out, you stop and face him.

Jacala Boy lunges off his board at you as the lip falls down vertically just above him. You shoot the nose of your board up at his face as you dive off the back.

b)

a)

You miss Nelly's leash as he drops into the wave. You watch, hoping he falls and the breaker creams him.

The barrel spits and Nelly comes riding over the back, his fists raised victoriously. His scores are raised—all quite high—then you see something that makes you want to vomit: a big red penalty marker has been raised against you!

"Damn it!" you curse, then slap the water in frustration. "I can't believe they saw that! I didn't even touch his leash! How can they count that as a penalty?"

Nelly strokes casually by you and says calmly: "Crime doesn't pay."

You reach out and grab the rail of his board, threatening to overturn him.

45

Your board resurfaces in pieces—the wave shattered it! You find the nose portion and ride it like a kickboard all the way to the beach.

On the sand, your shaper rushes up to you. Behind him is a famous shaper from the cutting-edge board company, Loopistix.

"What did you shape my board with?" you taunt your shaper. "Pretzels?!"

"That wave was heavy," he retorts, handing you a fresh board.

"Listen," the Loopistix shaper addresses you directly, "you've no more time to lose with another faulty stick. I want to sign you on, this instant. Just take one of my boards out now."

He barks up to his assistants, who skip down to the water's edge with several new Loopistix surfboards in their arms.

b)

a)

Suddenly the reef appears directly beneath you, perhaps only a foot below the surface!

"Good Lord!" you cry, praying the wave won't suck completely dry.

But your nightmares are confirmed with the sudden protrusion of massive coral heads at the barrel exit. You're considering punching through the back, but you know you will get sucked over the falls and slammed on the dry reef if you try it.

At the last second you grab your rails and redirect your line up toward the barrel's ceiling. You're completely upside-down when you look down at the base of the wave and see patches of craggy dry reef. But then you look to your right—where the lip is unloading—and feel a sudden spur of hope as you see the lip clearing the exposed coral and breaking into deeper water. Your only chance is to try to complete your impromptu barrel roll. You begin falling down with the lip . . .

46

Your skegs clear the coral head and you land the ollie in a smooth glide, then exit the gaping barrel. You speed over the top of the wave, raising your fists high in glory. You look in towards the beach and there above the judges' box are high points across the board, a 9.9 topping them off.

"Hey!" you hear someone call from the channel. It's a cameraman. "Hey!" he shouts. "I got that ollie on film! That was the sickest barrel ride I've ever seen! You're gonna clinch the world title!"

"Yes!" you shout rapturously, flashing him the shaka sign. You paddle back out to the lineup, and it's not long until the others rejoin you.

b)

a)

The shark drags you underwater and begins chewing on your leg in earnest, thrashing you from side to side. In desperation, you jam two fingers into its left eye with all your might. The shark immediately releases its grip and you swim away from its monstrous jaws towards the surface.

You claw ever upwards, seeing sunlight and your red blood adrift in the water. You feel as if you're going to black out. You're desperate for oxygen—but you don't give up.

At last you reach the surface and take a massive gulp of air. Your board is nearby, so you swim to it, then sit up on it to get a better look at your leg.

47

Unfortunately you're nowhere near the channel when the whitewater hits you. You try to duck-dive but immediately get hammered by a violent swirl of turbulence that tears your board from your hands, snaps your leash and tumbles you head over heels all the way to the beach.

Your wash up and can't find your board. You walk a few paces up the beach and scan the frothy inside.

Just then, Jacala Boy delivers a hard kick to your ribs.

"Aaw!" you cry as your face eats the sand. You hop to your feet and slink away, a sharp pain shooting along your side. You see him coming at you with his fists raised, so you hold your fists in front of you as best you can. He takes a heavy swing at your head.

b)

The End

You fight to swim out the back, but the wave sucks you into the falls! You feel weightless, then descend quickly towards the shallow reef. You brace yourself for the impact, but it feels futile, like you are merely a single pea in a massive pouring of split-pea soup.

The wave smashes you legs-first into the reef and your body folds, whipping your head against the stone-solid reef. Your skull cracks open and salt water leaks into your brain.

Jacala Boy makes it out of the Backdoor barrel to win a high-scoring ride. But for you everything has gone black.

48

You look over your board carefully. Jacala knocked the two side skegs out cleanly. The back skeg is still solidly in place. You decide to keep competing with your board as a single-fin.

You paddle back out and take your position beside Nelly.

b)

Heads - Page 39b   **Flip a coin**   **Tails - Page 71a**

a)

Jacala Boy keeps tugging at your jersey, so you sock him in the jaw. He falls into the trough with a violent splash. When you look forward again, the lip is already pitching out far ahead as the second tube section takes form. There's a loud sucking sound as the cylindrical barrel squeezes a roomful of air inside its wide belly. You hold your line, but as the lip cascades down further and further ahead of you, you fear you might be too deep.

Suddenly you hear an otherworldly roar and feel a strong, continuous blast of wind at your back. The barrel is spitting, driving out all that compressed air. The power of the escaping air and mist is like the exhaust from a jet engine, and it blows you forward in a hazardous fashion. You teeter over the nose of your board, losing your balance.

49

"Aaaaah!" Jacala Boy screams as the nose of your board pierces his eye, then the wave detonates on you both, obliterating your reality.

"Yaaaaah!" Jacala Boy screams. You've resurfaced right into him! He's bearing down on you with one empty eye socket spilling blood everywhere!

"My eye!" he howls in pain. "You poken out ma eye! I gonna kill you!"

You try to push him off, but his cumbersome body is too heavy and he is intent on revenge. He dunks you under time and time again, and every time you emerge you see the same horrible sight: the bloody Hawaiian with the empty eye socket. His stringy black locks shadow the sun as he tries to drown you. You claw back at him desperately, then reach for his face.

b)

a)

Your skegs catch on the coral head and you go flying forward off your board over the shallowest part of the trough and into deeper water. But the wave gives you a fierce beating—you're pounded to your limit.

You finally reach the surface and take a huge gulp of life-giving oxygen. You're dizzy from the wipeout, but unharmed. There are no more waves coming, so you bob near the inside for a moment to regain your bearings. You don't feel the slightest pull on your leash, so you look around for your board, worried it might be broken.

50

"Alright Jacala Boy," you reply diplomatically, letting go of the green tortoise. "Just pipe down."

He resumes paddling back towards the lineup, glaring back with stony eyes beneath heavy brows.

Nelly paddles by. He looks at you with raised brows.

"Don't ask," you quip, as you follow in his wake to the lineup.

"Hey, lighten up, JB," Nelly intercedes. "Let's just compete and have fun, okay?"

Jacala Boy's fierce expression soon gives way to a waxing smile. He shakes his head and replies: "Fun at Pipe, brah. K den, we cool."

You are relieved.

b)

a)

Suddenly the shark's mouth opens wide, exposing rows of teeth. It clamps down on your leg, taking it clean off.

You scream underwater, your bubbles of precious oxygen rising to the surface. You try to struggle upwards, but you're in shock—nauseous and dizzy. Every time you try to kick, you expect to feel the resistance of water against both feet propelling you forward. But one of your legs is missing. It's an eerie and sick feeling.

The surface is far away and shock has got the better of you. You begin to feel comfortable in your new underwater realm. Maybe it's no longer worth fighting to get to the surface.

51

As the first wave prepares to throw, you toy with the idea of going for it. It's a truly humongous wave. You take a few strokes from the lip, just to see how the water carries you. If momentum comes quickly, you may very well commit.

b)

a)

You precariously cross paths with Nelly and JB as you make it to the bottom of the wave—but there is not enough room for each of you to bottom turn. You and your rivals struggle to pull up into the barrel as the lip comes down like a guillotine. Will the lip let you under, into the safety of the barrel, or will it cream all three of you like bananas in a blender?

52

A sharp pain shoots up your leg.

"Aaaaah!" you scream in agony, then look down to see a stonefish swimming away. The pain is like nothing you've ever felt. It's acute and extreme. You look at your foot. Six pinholes mark where you have been stung.

You begin to swim in, but soon grow nauseous and dizzy. You stop for a moment to catch your breath. You continue with a backstroke and immediately begin vomiting uncontrollably. You stop swimming and are overcome with shivers as your pulse rate skyrockets—the venom is now circulating through your bloodstream. You black out for a few seconds, then come to. You struggle to focus on the shoreline. You see the water patrol setting out for you, then everything goes black forever. You are not revived.

The End

a)

"No!" you protest, yanking the IV from your arm and springing off the stretcher.

The medics and water patrol try to surround you, but you outmaneuver them and run over to a lifeguard tower, where a tri-fin longboard is leaning against the stilts.

"Hey!" the lifeguard shouts as you grab his board. "What do you think you're doing with my board?"

"I'm going for the world title!" you shout back.

"You gonna rush it on my rescue board?" he yells. "Don't think so, bro!"

You lunge forward onto the board and paddle hard seaward.

53

As you struggle back onto your board, Nelly spins around and catches the large breaker. You dizzily float over the crest, watching him dart down into the pit. He digs his whole arm into the wave to slow down, and then the liquid curtain covers him. You look outside and there are no more waves coming.

You see Nelly rocket out into the channel and raise his fists high in glory. You shake your head, but then, squinting at the scoreboard, you do a double take: Nelly scored zero points! Above the list of zeroes you can make out the following words in red: "Interference Disqualification."

"Ha ha!" you hoot and clap. "They saw him shove me! They saw that!"

Nelly paddles back out. Vengeance now reigns at the Pipeline.

b)

a)

Nelly gets past you just as the wave starts to pitch. You see him stand up and shoot down the face. You drop in, too, then crank a bottom turn and ride just behind him. But as the barrel takes shape overhead, he stalls, stuffing you in the pit.

You have two choices: either stall as well and hope to make it out on his heels, or keep your speed and try to pass him in the narrow tube. If you collide with him while attempting the pass, you'll both wipe out and the interference call will be on you. But if he stuffs you too deep in the pit, you might not make it out of the barrel.

54

You can't fight the pull of the heaving Backdoor lip. It sucks you up and over the falls, slamming you into the base of the wave with overwhelming power. You guard your head with your arms as you tumble in avalanches of whitewater. Miraculously you do not hit the reef.

You resurface with water spilling out of your nose and ears. You see your board nearby, retrieve it, and sprint-paddle out of the impact zone, towards the outside. When you finally turn to read the scoreboard, you're totally enraged. Jacala Boy scored a perfect ten!

"You cheat!" you yell towards him.

"Ay, rookie!" he calls in your direction. "Watch what you say, eh?"

Your nerves are strung tight. You look at Nelly and can tell he's peeved. You paddle a good twenty yards away from Jacala Boy. Each of you scans the horizon for another set.

b)

a)

"Back off, sport," Nelly quips.

You glance outside and see another set approaching. You tip Nelly over and shove his head underwater. Your equilibrium is shaky as you paddle with all your might, then hop to your feet. Your board catches air and you dive off to the side, freefalling from four stories up.

Oh crap, you think as you brace for the impact.

Instead of penetrating the water, you bounce off the surface and then the heavy lip practically knocks the life out of you. You get pummeled underwater and have no idea which way is up or down. When the terrible spinning stops, you're able to see daylight some eighteen feet above. You're surprised the water can be this deep at Pipe, but soon realize you've been drilled into a hole.

55

You make it to the bottom of the wave. Nelly and Jacala Boy crisscross one another dangerously as they negotiate their bottom turns. You see the Pipeline lip—sharp, heavy and fast—falling down at them. Realizing they will both get axed, you bottom turn to the right, away from them, towards Backdoor. You barely make it under a vertical lip and into a gaping barrel. It's unclear if the tube will stay open. There are ugly boils everywhere in the trough, and the wave looks like it's going to close out.

b)

a)

Both you and Nelly get mopped up by the whitewater.

You tuck your arms and legs in as you tumble, and then—Conk! Your head hits a rounded clump of reef. You reach the surface seconds later and climb onto your board. You see Nelly's board nearby, but there is no sign of Nelly himself.

Another large wave breaks and the whitewater begins loping towards you. You're torn between finding Nelly and saving your own skin. You don't want to get drilled again, so you paddle swiftly towards the channel, just squeaking by the rumbling whitewater.

You turn again, looking for Nelly. But now you don't even see his board.

56

You paddle way outside, far beyond Pipeline's outer reef, then around to the west. Further to the west a massive wave rises like a mountain over the outer reef known as Himalayas. The wave breaks, throwing a barrel so big it could swallow a 737 airplane. You look on in awe.

Spectators watch you from the beach through binoculars. Photographers from all the surf magazines train their telephoto lenses on you.

"What on earth is the lunatic doing?" says a water patrolman on shore.

Oahu lifeguard and surfing hero Buck Quiggly answers: "The contestant is going all in, with life and limb."

By now you are within a few hundred yards of where the wave breaks. Heavy currents tug you this way and that, so you paddle more strongly towards the uncertain lineup in the distant open seas.

b)

a)

With Jacala Boy out of the way, you clamber back onto your board and paddle out towards Nelly. The noise of the fins cracking under Jacala's hand won't leave your mind. You notice your board paddles differently with only the back fin remaining, but there's no reason why you can't keep charging Pipeline. After all, Pipeline legends like Johnny Daring surfed big Pipe for years on single fins—and exceptionally well, at that.

"What?" Nelly says in disbelief as he watches Jacala Boy being carried up the beach by the water patrol. "What's wrong with JB?" he inquires, but you don't respond, you just keep paddling far beyond the six-time world champ. You are headed way out the back. You're through monkeying around with other competitors. You have your sights on catching a Third Reef bomb to clinch the win. With your focus on the blue horizon, you keep paddling.

57

You try to get up, but can't. You've been strapped to the stretcher.

"Here we are at the Pipe Masters event!" you hear a television commentator bleat into a microphone. "One of the finalists is now officially out of the contest due to injury. Would you like to comment on what happened out there?" he asks, thrusting his microphone into your face.

"Out of the contest?" you quip. "Nooo!" you cry, trying to wrench free. "I'm going back out there!"

"Sorry, hero," a medic says, "but you're going to the hospital."

"Well, folks," the media impresario turns to the cameras, "as you can see, a key contender in the Pipe Masters competition is down and out; and such a shame, so early in the event. This contest really separates the pros from the rookies . . ." he rambles on as you are loaded into an ambulance and sped away.

The End

a)

Suddenly, two tall coral heads pop up out of the water right in front of you. There's no way you can avoid them—you're going too fast. You aim your board between them and make it through!

You race into deeper water, crank a hard bottom turn, then slash the wave face as the monstrous barrel explodes to a close behind you.

"Wooo-hooo!" you hoot as you complete your spray-throwing carves. You ride up and over the shoulder, then lie back down on your board.

You look back at the scoreboard and see a row of high 9's, with one 10.

Feeling like Neptune's firstborn, you conspicuously stretch your arm and neck muscles, then paddle nonchalantly back towards the lineup.

58

All too soon, the first wave of the set bores down on you. You try to hold on to Jacala Boy, but the powerful whitewater rips him from your clutches.

Noooooo! you scream in your mind as you fight to hold your breath. The chaotic beating you are suffering spells serious trouble for JB, whose fate may be sealed in Pipeline's washing machine.

Kaboom, kaboom, you hear as you emerge from the whitewater. Those explosions can only mean one thing: two more set waves have broken in quick succession and are now rushing towards you. You scan the surface for Jacala Boy before diving under again. You're filled with intense grief: you can't find JB.

b)

a)

You're situated on the outside now. A nice-looking set jacks up. You're in perfect position for the first wave. Nelly and Jacala Boy are soon jockeying around you.

"This is my wave, bruddahs!" Jacala sneers. He begins stroking for it, his body torquing from side to side like a snake.

"Not so fast JB!" Nelly retorts, as he squirrels his way into the wave.

"Chaa!" you ridicule in disgust, letting the snakes have their way.

Jacala Boy gets caught up in the lip and pulls back, while Nelly gets a high-scoring tube ride. Jacala Boy, still deeper than you, picks off the second wave. There's only one wave left—a small, frothy one. You turn and begin paddling for it, then smile when you see Jacala Boy caught inside—he wiped out!

59

Nelly is unable to streak by you. You paddle into the wave and aim vertically down the face as the lip begins to pitch. Suddenly, to your great alarm, the wave buckles inward and your board loses contact with the wave. You are now freefalling towards the trough. You feel the wind rushing up around you and are still centered over your board. You've made a few airdrops like this before, but never at Pipe. You stay focused and try to land the drop.

b)

a)

You look back and forth from your shaper to the Loopistix rep. Your shaper's expression is one of disbelief, as he realizes you are seriously considering dumping him.

"We can offer you a loopi-lucrative contract," the Loopistix rep says.

"For how many years? And give me some cash figures."

"But, but . . ." your shaper stutters, "don't you like my boards?"

"We can't ring out figures here," the rep says. "Just take any one of my boards out and consider it a deal. I promise you won't be disappointed. You'll love our new Superloops design. Trust me."

"Sorry, I would need it in writing," you reply, then grab your shaper's board and paddle back outside.

60

The nose of your board misses Jacala's face by less than an inch, then the heavy Backdoor lip hits, pummeling you both horrendously. You're driven down fast and are surprised not to slam into the reef—after all, this is shallow Backdoor. Then you realize what's going on . . .

Backdoor Pipeline has one deep hole in its otherwise shallow reef, and this hole leads to an underwater cave where many a surfer has been trapped and died. You fight for the surface with renewed vigor!

Finally, you reach the surface and take a deep breath. But that first breath is strangely musty. You open your eyes and everything is dark. "Hello!" you say, and it echoes off the walls of the underwater cave.

b)

a)

You keep paddling all the way to Outer Logs—a famous North Shore big-wave break. The media helicopter leaves the Pipeline arena and begins circling over you. Now the media and spectators are watching you, exclusively.

Outer Logs is huge and glassy. It looks rideable—if you can paddle hard enough to get into the wave.

You sit up on your board and wait for a big set, focusing intently on the horizon. The water surges and swells beneath you. In the realm of the open ocean, you feel as miniscule as an ant. But you know that if you can bag just one Outer Logs monster, you'll win the Pipe Masters competition easily.

You look down into the dark depths and your mind starts to spook you. What large sea-creatures dwell beneath? Suddenly, the water splashes up just beside you!

61

You're unable to spin your body around with the barrel. Unlike a cat, you can't right yourself before you land. You fall headfirst with the lip, still holding the rails of your board. The last thing you see is a massive coral head rising up out of the water.

Your cranium splits over the coral head.

Then, in a freaky display, your body shoots up out of the churning whitewater. The photographers capture forever what the crowd sees: your body, from your feet up, ends at your lower jaw. Everything above the jaw is obliterated. Many scream in horror. If only you could hear them . . . If only you weren't dead.

The End

a)

Your frustration turns to near insanity. You choke the turtle more vigorously, ignoring Jacala Boy's warnings. The sea creature which once got in your way looks up at you sadly, emits a final, choking gasp, then its eyes close and its head falls limp.

"Aaaaaah!" Jacala Boy screams, fuming with anger. "You gonna die now brah!" He paddles toward you at full speed, revenge spiking his eyes, lips drawn tight.

You let go of the turtle's neck and it slowly sinks—but then it starts swimming away.

Jacala is getting closer. You abandon all hope of talking diplomatically and paddle like hell to get away from him. You angle in towards the reef, hoping to catch a wave.

"It's all ova for you, brah!" JB warns as he paddles rapidly in your wake.

62

You're mad as hell and quickly climb back onto your board, but as soon as you're on it, Nelly socks you in the face. All this time the wave is jacking ever higher.

"Damn punk!" you curse, shaking the dizziness from your head.

You see Nelly turn sharply and begin paddling for the wave. You reach out and grab his leash again, pulling on it with all you've got. This redirects you in line with him. You feel the wave rising sharply beneath you, and you are now both equal before the drop. However, by pulling on his leash, you significantly slowed his momentum and gave yourself some forward thrust. You're still a bit discombobulated, but you decide to just go for it. Nelly strokes hard beside you, trying to keep pace. You ignore him, hop to your feet and rocket down the face. You almost pearl, but make the drop in beautiful form.

b)

a)

The first wave strikes all too soon. A swimming pool's worth of water throws from the lip and explodes before you with terrible force. A mountain of whitewater rushes at you like a landslide. You push Jacala Boy towards the channel, then dive under before the great white snowball of doom plows over you.

You get thrashed something fierce, like a voodoo doll being whipped about in a dog's jaws. When you reach the surface, you immediately scan the channel for Jacala Boy. He made it!

You swim over to him, but find him floating face-down, motionless. You begin rescue breaths, then CPR as best you can. Nelly arrives moments later to help.

Cuuuh-Cuuh! Jacala Boy coughs up saltwater.

"You're gonna make it, Jacala Boy!" you shout in encouragement. "Just hang in there!"

63

Just then, something seizes you by the arms. At first you think it's the shark, but then you look up to see Jacala Boy struggling to pull you towards daylight. You reach the surface and inhale a great breath of air. Jacala Boy has saved you, but not your leg. It's been bitten off.

"C'mon, brah!" he yells forcefully as he swims you towards the beach. "Just hang in there! No maki die dead, brah! You can make it!"

The pain in your leg has all but disappeared. You are going into shock.

"Squeeze yo leg!" Jacala Boy demands. "It will slow da bleeding!"

You reach down and squeeze your leg above the stump, and soon feel dry sand on your back.

b)

a)

This is a heavy wave indeed. You look left and the lip is warbled—you fear it will do something unexpected if you try to drop in. You also see your competitors there, looking first left, then right. As the wave surges up, Nelly backs out. You look right.

"Eh try move, brah!" Jacala shouts from behind you. "Comin' down!"

64

You manage to keep your balance and hold your line. After the blast of wind, the entire barrel is filled with a drifting mist, but you can see the clear blue lip forming a beautiful barrel all around you. Soon you feel the sun on your face and see it sparkling off the water, giving the illusion of rainbow diamonds everywhere you look. You glide out of the big blue cylinder, smiling from ear to ear, then kick out the back of the wave victoriously.

You turn to view your scores and they are not long in coming: all high 9's, and one 10!

"Woooo-hooo!" you hoot, absolutely stoked. Now you really feel like you can clinch this contest. You paddle back out, totally amped.

b)

a)

"Ouch!" you cry, as you feel a dozen sharp needles pierce the bottom of your left foot.

You raise your foot out of the water and become nauseous when you see a spiny black sea urchin stuck to the bottom of your foot. Every slight movement of the urchin sends unbearable shocks of pain up your leg, and you almost faint. You realize that unless you remove the urchin from your foot right now, you will be unable to compete further. There's not enough time to go in and undergo treatment by meticulous medics.

You brace yourself as best you can and count down to the decisive moment of extraction: "Three – two – one!"

65

"Whoa there!" Nelly says, paddling up beside you. "You okay?"

"Not really," you reply with a glum expression. You lift your leg out of the water, and he winces at the sight. Your leg is chewed up pretty bad, like a chainsaw has bounced off it a few times. Just looking at it makes you nauseous.

Suddenly, a rogue wave marches in fast, swinging wide. You decide to catch it. As you paddle for the towering wall of water, Nelly looks at you and shakes his head, no.

You stroke hard, then get to your feet. Your stance is unsteady as you look down the face—but it's too late to back out: you're committed.

b)

a)

"What's the contract?" you ask, giving the Loopistix boards a serious scanning over.

"Five hundred thousand for this contest," the Loopistix rep says, "even if you don't win, you'll still get the money. Next year, two million, and the year after that, three million. And all the boards you want. It's a three-year deal. I have the contract right here," he adds, pulling a circular document from a portfolio.

"Okay," you decide. "I'll take it . . . as long as you give me one million if I win this contest."

The Loopistix rep scribbles a new number on the contract and hands it to you with his ballpoint pen.

Your shaper looks on in total disbelief as you drop his board and tell him he's fired. You sign the new contract, grab a fresh Loopistix stick, then rush back out to the lineup.

66

After a long wait, a set finally comes. But for some reason the wave faces are all warbled. You decide to go for the first one. It's smaller than the ones behind it, but it's got better shape. You know that catching a large Pipeline wave with a significant cross-chop is a recipe for disaster. The others willingly let you have the first roller. Jacala Boy even laughs at you.

"Ha ha ha!" he sneers. "Good luck!"

The wave is only about eight foot on the face, but fast. You rocket down and stick your bottom turn, then you see a three-foot cross-chop heading right towards you. It's a perfect ramp. You set your line right at it, preparing to do a sick air.

b)

a)

Suddenly gnarled clumps of reef pop up out of the water everywhere around you.

"Good Lord!" you exclaim.

67

Just then, you are seized from above. You look up and make out Jacala Boy pulling you towards the surface. You watch his feet kick as he struggles to move your body upwards. There are bubbles all around you and billows of red water. You glimpse Jacala Boy's tattoos and Bermuda trunks. Then you lose the energy to look up.

You stare down, into the red and darkness. The greatest light you have—your life—suddenly switches off. All is black.

The End

a)

So far, so good: you're pulling yourself out of the barrel-roll like a cat righting itself from an upside-down fall. You wrest your board around, forcing it under your feet, then freefall the remainder of the loop in good form. You connect with water again and are immediately thrown off balance, but you're able to stay on your board and complete the maneuver. The crowd roars.

"Incredible!" the MC exclaims over the loudspeaker. "Ladies and gentlemen! This is a first in surfing history! A finalist at the Pipe Master's competition has just completed a barrel roll at Backdoor Pipeline!"

As the beachside fanfare continues to rollick, you glance in to see your score . . .

68

"I wouldn't do anything stupid, if I were you," Nelly warns. He then spits in your face.

"Two-faced bastard!" you curse as you tilt him off his board.

"Warning! Warning!" the loudspeakers blare. "Sabotaging your opponent is cause for disqualification from the contest!"

"Stuff it!" you yell back at the judges. You lift Nelly's board high out of the water for all to see and break it in half over your head. You toss the pieces back at Nelly, then flick off the judges and laugh.

"You are disqualified!" the loudspeakers blare. "Come in at once, or be forced in!"

You see a contingent of burly Hawaiian locals entering the water. Your equilibrium is still out of whack and you're feeling dizzy. Fact is, you're history.

The End

a)

You can't keep your balance—you dive off the front of your board . . . But from the beach it looks spectacular! You come rocketing out of the barrel like Superman in flight before diving safely underneath the wave.

You resurface and scan the scoreboard. A few high 7's come up, with one 8!

"Eh brah!" you hear Jacala Boy scream.

You sigh to yourself and mumble, "The mad dog is at it again."

"Eh brah!" he screams again. "Where you goin?"

You don't look back, you just keep paddling deeper into the lineup. A walled-up set looms on the horizon.

69

You pump twice for speed, which is enough to send you racing past him— but not before nicking his shoulder, causing both of you to go off balance. You teeter on your board as the thick lip falls beside you like a heavy waterfall with not a drop of water out of place. As you struggle to keep your balance, you see Nelly behind you doing the same: he is arching his back and twirling his arms, trying not to fall into the guillotine of crystalline water.

As the barrel begins to narrow with both of you still inside, you lean out of control towards the lip. The glass axe passes ever closer to your face. You lean and counterlean, trying to get your balance. Which way will you lean now? Towards the exit of the barrel, or towards the blade-like lip?

b)

The End

BAM! Jacala Boy's punch connects and everything goes black.

You wake up in a hospital, time and location unknown. The entire side of your head is swollen and you have a terrible headache. You grab a remote from the bedside table and turn on the TV. *Hawaii Five-O* is just beginning.

Is that Pipeline? you wonder, watching the wave at the start of the program.

Just then, a nurse walks in and turns off the TV. Brandishing a long thermometer, she says: "Time to take your temperature. Roll over."

70

You feel your board connect again with the water at the base of the wave. You landed a sick airdrop, but are having difficulty holding your balance. You spin your arms to keep from falling, as the thick Pipeline lip comes down.

"No!" you cry, as your board goes squirrelly and out of control. It's not riding responsively.

You fight to regain your balance by widening your stance. If this works you could thrust a quick bottom turn and make it under the lip. But if it doesn't— it's going to be painful!

b)

Heads - Page 92a   **Flip a coin**   **Tails - Page 98a**

Heads - Page 95b   **Flip a coin**   **Tails - Page 101b**

a)

After a long wait, a set finally comes. It's stacking up on the horizon, so you head for the outside. Nelly takes off on the third wave, as you paddle over it. Then a magnificent wave peaks before you; it's a sheet of blue glass, glowing like tourmaline.

You turn around and stroke into it, then jump to your feet and begin to make the drop. The ramp is easy and you are in total control—so much so, in fact, that you decide to try a 360 on your single fin. You turn your nose sharply up the wall and it begins to slide all the way around, completing the circle.

What a mind-blowing maneuver, you think. I'll clinch the contest for sure! But as you complete the 360, you catch your inside rail! You bend your knees to force the 360 through. You know if you can just pull this off, the world title will be yours!

71

Jacala Boy grasps your neck and chokes you as you attempt to push him away. He blocks your windpipe completely, and your face turns blue. You feel like you're going to black out, so out of desperation you jam your thumb into Jacala Boy's good eye.

"Yeeeaaaaoooowww!" he screams in agony, blood spurting from his eye socket. Your tactic works—he releases his grip. He places his hands over his bloody eyes and has difficulty staying afloat.

Suddenly another wave explodes right into you both.

b)

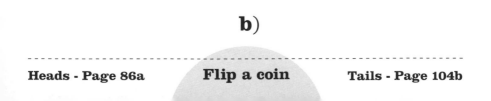

Heads - Page 86a   **Flip a coin**   **Tails - Page 104b**

a)

The lip falls further ahead and you fade further back inside a warping tube. You navigate through the bending barrel on your stiff and unresponsive board. To your dismay, you're fading too deep.

Suddenly, in a strong gust of offshore trade winds, the barrel exit slows down and widens, staying open just long enough for you to make it out. You race ahead of the tube and ride over the top of the wave, kicking out. Your board is not turning well. But looking back to see your score, you can only smile—all high numbers, one being a 9.8!

Nelly is paddling hard back to the lineup, and Jacala Boy is swimming in, holding the side of his head. He is without his board.

You remove your side skegs to give you looser turning in the style of a single-fin, then paddle back towards the lineup.

72

You slowly stand up in the cave, take a deep breath, and carefully feel the walls. You're overcome with fear when you realize there are several coral tunnels leading in unknown directions. Finding your way out in the dark will not be easy.

You decide to follow the largest molehole—a conduit in which you can almost stand up straight. You feel your way through. It's slow going in the dark—you don't want to bump your head or step into a crag your foot would get stuck in.

You round a corner and see a faint light ahead. You walk towards the light and soon you can see the gnarled coral that surrounds you. Crabs and mollusks hide in the honeycombed walls. There is one final corner to turn before you see the source of the light—what you pray will be an exit large enough for you to fit through. You hear a low sloshing of water and see patterns of reflecting light before you, then your eyes widen in astonishment at what you find . . .

b)

a)

You rocket down towards Jacala Boy.

"Look out, brah!" he screams up at you.

You deliberately slice right next to him before cranking a smooth bottom turn. The frothy whitewater wave moves extra fast as it barrels into shape. You casually put your hands behind your hips and take a ride through the green room, exiting before it closes. You glance back towards the scoreboard and see high 9's and one 10! You let out a sharp whistle before joining Nelly and Jacala back in the lineup.

"This board rides like a dream!" you tell Nelly, then add: "Pipe is best without a gang of locals!"

Jacala Boy, the local, wears a sour expression.

73

Heading to the outside, you feel good about your decisive action. The longboard paddles fast and sure, and seems like it will turn well. It's about ten feet in length. You're guaranteed to get a ton of waves on it. You have lots of experience on a log, and even more on a modern design of this kind.

You stop and take a moment to attach the board's leash to your ankle. You're not sure you want to be attached to such a large board, but you don't want a dragging leash to slow you down, and you don't want to give your competitors something to yank at as you're going for a wave.

You keep paddling, more confident than ever that you can still clinch the world title.

b)

a)

There's still a current underwater; it's holding you down. You struggle to swim up against it, but make little headway. You don't know how much longer you'll be able to hold out.

Out of desperation, you reach down to your ankle and grab the end of your leash. Then you begin climbing towards the surface, hand over hand, like a cheating rock climber.

You reach the tail end of your board to discover it is also underwater—only the top two feet remain above the surface. Your board is tombstoning. You grab the rails and begin to climb towards the nose. You're only a few feet from the surface and precious oxygen!

74

The risk in trying to pass Nelly seems too great, so you ride up as close as you can behind him and stall, just like he is doing. As huge section after huge section continues to fall down in front of him, you simply follow his lead. Eventually you see him pump for speed and exit the tube. At this point, you stall at the barrel exit, effectively shielding yourself from the crowd's view. Then, just before the bowl implodes, you shoot forth into daylight. A spitting mist blows over your back and the crowd erupts in cheers. You do a flying kick over the back of the wave, grinning at Nelly from ear to ear. He scores in the mid-nine range, while your scores are slightly higher.

"What!" Nelly cries, but not at the scores—he is watching a massive set build over the reef. The safety of the channel is far, far away. There's no way around it: you're both caught inside!

b)

The End

The crowd on the beach gasps as you aim down the face of a steep Pipeline beast. You drive down, then start your bottom turn. Your leg gives out, causing you to fly off your board. You get sucked up and over into a freefall. You fight to swim out the back, but it's too late. Now you're freefalling! You brace for impact. The last thing you hear is a loud crack!

The water patrol immediately see there's a problem. Your board is broken in half and the tail end is tombstoning. They race out on the Jet Ski and pull you up to the surface by your leash. Your skull is cracked open and you're unconscious. They race you to shore and call to the medics for help. The medics try to revive you, but are unable to. Your head hit the reef, with fatal consequences.

The winner of the Pipe Masters contest made big news for a few days. But your can-do attitude, gusto, and courageous last ride are talked about in surfing circles for years to come. You lose the contest, but die a hero.

75

Ouuh! is the noise of Jacala Boy getting taken out by the lip behind you. Ahead you see Nelly turn hard towards the face, so you do likewise. The lip tags your shoulder, but you make it under the curtain and ride the barrel with Nelly.

Suddenly, Nelly stalls. It seems he's purposefully trying to stuff you, but you'd rather collide into him than allow this to happen—better that both of you don't make it than just you. You rocket past him, brushing his shoulder.

Once ahead of him, you consider giving him a taste of his own medicine: stalling in the pit, thereby stuffing him. After all, he's riding far back in the barrel. It could be so easy.

b)

Heads - Page 5b   **Flip a coin**   **Tails - Page 8a**

a)

The next thing you know, medics are lifting you onto a stretcher and putting you in an ambulance. The doors remain open as they tend to your stump. As they stick an IV into your arm, you hear a voice from afar.

"Try wait!" the voice wails. It's Jacala Boy Bones. "We got da leg! We found da leg!"

"Here!" a medic beside you yells. "Toss it here!"

Jacala Boy flings your leg into the ambulance. At the end of that leg is your foot, which kicks you in the face as the medic makes the catch. He looks down at you and says "ouch," then places your leg in an ice chest. The ambulance speeds off with sirens blaring.

76

Waves keep rolling in, pounding the area in which Nelly went down and increasing your anxiety. Not wanting to swim into the impact zone, you leave that job to the water patrol.

You paddle about eighty yards further out before swinging into a nice looking breaker. The lip races towards you like a slingshot. You pop up, aim down the face, then bottom turn into a cavernous barrel. You are slotted for a second, then bait fish begin to rain out of the top of the barrel. Hundreds of them pelt you like soft bullets. You shield your eyes with your hands. You exit the barrel, a violent spitting wind driving the little fish against your back. The air horn sounds the end of the heat. You score a 10, a 9.9, and a few 9.7's! You're stoked that you made it through that bizarre ride.

When you get to shore, you see a circle of medics surrounding Nelly. You walk closer and see that your rival's body is blue and the rescue crew are desperately giving him CPR. You keep walking towards the judges' box and grandstand.

b)

a)

Smack! You blast off the watery lip, then grab your rail and twist your torso, forcing yourself through a 360. You land it successfully on the wave. But as you kick out, you slice your left foot badly on your skeg.

"Ouch!" you howl in pain as you paddle back out. You glance back and see two 9.8s, which helps to ease the pain. You take your position in the lineup beside Nelly, who excitedly inquires about your aerial.

You answer nonchalantly: "I just saw this little ramp coming, so I aimed right at it and launched. When I first got lift, I realized I would have some hang time to work with, so I went ahead and did a 360. It was pretty basic, really. But I cut my foot kicking out, and it's killing me!"

77

You set a fast pace to the outside reefs, intent on catching a few true Third Reef bombs before the contest ends. You want to clinch the win. But suddenly you realize you're not alone . . .

A giant fin breaks the surface only a few yards away! The fin is bigger than anything you have ever seen. Bigger than the fin in the movie *Jaws*. It stands easily five feet out of the water. Your heart is pumping hard.

The fin angles sharply down into the water as the body of a whale rises and blows a spout high into the sky. A whale that has rolled to the surface! You're relieved it wasn't a shark, but relief turns instantly to fear as the creature raises its humongous tail directly over your head.

b)

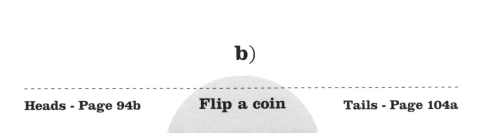

a)

To your dismay, a mix of water patrolmen, lifeguards, and some seaworthy medics pursues you into the surf on longboards. There must be a dozen of them, and most are fitter than Arnold Schwarzenegger. They're stroking hard to catch you, but you still have a good lead.

You see a large set rising over the outer reefs and know that if you can catch a wave, it will prove to everybody that you're in good enough condition to surf. Jacala Boy and Nelly watch as the gang of watermen paddle out with poor timing while the big set approaches.

"Ah ha ha," you laugh, paddling towards Backdoor to better evade your pursuers.

The gang stroke furiously to get over the approaching set. You won't mind seeing them get creamed by a Backdoor bomb.

78

Most of the spines break off in your foot as you try to remove the urchin.

"Aoowww!" you howl in agony as you look at the bottom of your foot. It's blue and swollen, with red spots of blood welling up around the broken spikes.

"Shoot! Shoot Shoot!" you exclaim in pain. Your eyes are watering from the fiery nails driven into your sole, and you know you won't be able to continue surfing.

With some hesitation, you make your way back to shore. Medics meet you on the sand and carry you to a tent. They numb your foot, then begin the slow process of digging out the spines. You lie there and watch your opponents catching waves. They are still working on your foot when Nelly Yater takes the winner's platform.

The End

a)

You fall off your board and begin to cartwheel down the face of the wave as it jacks up higher and higher. The wipeout is hideous. You are drilled to the reef below and held there by massive downward pressure. You become desperate for air. You try to push off the reef, but the water forces you right back down.

This is it—you're just about out of breath. You decide to quit fighting against the heavy water and go with it instead—it's your only hope to conserve the last of your air. You go into Zen mode, slightly opening your arms and legs and trying to let your muscles relax. The whitewater throws you like a rag doll. As your feet slam into the reef, you pray your head will not do the same. Your time window to surface is quickly closing . . .

79

You rise over the first wave and look down about forty feet at some water patrolmen all caught inside.

Kaboom! The wave detonates right on top of them. You laugh hysterically.

A second wave rises beneath you. You look down and see a mess of boards and bodies struggling for the surface. The second wave slams into them again, cleaning them up and washing them ashore.

A third wave jacks up over the reef. You catch it and bottom turn into a massive Backdoor bowl. A water photographer raises his camera in front of you. Will you be featured on the cover of next month's *Ocean Surf Magazine*?

b)

a)

You deflect Jacala Boy's punch, but in doing so you fall back onto the sand.

He lifts his foot above your head and stomps hard. You dodge the blow. He stomps again. This time you roll. When he lifts his foot for the third time, you grab his other leg and bring him down. You spring to your feet.

"Stop right there!" says a burly Hawaiian lifeguard. "Stop da fight now or you both go a jail!"

You look at the lifeguard, then back at JB. You want to slam your knee full-force into Jacala Boy's gut. You look back to the lifeguard and say, "Sorry, brah. This fight ain't over."

80

Your leg almost gives out as you make the drop. The crowd on the beach stands in suspense. The heavy Pipeline lip comes down fast, but not before you get under it.

Seconds later you glide out of the gaping barrel. The crowd erupts in robust hooting and applause as you race across the flats. The air horn blasts the official end of the contest.

On the beach you are surrounded by both media and medics. The former shove microphones in your face, while the latter practically mummify you in bandages. Your bros carry you up to the stage, where your rivals arrive a few minutes later. But it's you who is sprayed with champagne as you hold the golden trophy above your head! You win!

The End

a)

"Aaaaah!" you hear Nelly exclaim behind you as the lip hits him, taking him out.

Now Jacala Boy turns sharply up the wave face. The lip covers him perfectly, but comes down on your head.

The impact knocks you off your board and you get sucked back up into the wave. You attempt to swim out the back and are able to punch through, but your leash is taut at your ankle. The wave has your board and it's pulling you back into the maelstrom.

81

You've scored a perfect 10! That is to say, every single judge has given you a 10!

"Woooo-hoo!" you shout in glee, feeling like you have clinched the world title.

You line up outside and your competitors paddle up beside you. They are angered, frustrated, and amazed at your score. A set comes and you all paddle for the first roller. It's a beautiful wave—glassy and perfect. It looks like it will have an easy drop and a big tube. This wave could seal the title for you. Nelly and Jacala try hard to outmaneuver you. They can't let you get any more points. The wave is beginning to pitch as all three of you catch it and stand up.

b)

a)

You paddle hard and make it to the Third Reef area with a decent amount of time left in the contest.

This is it, you tell yourself. I just need to bag one of these big daddys to clinch the contest.

You don't have to wait long. A big set marches in from the open ocean. The first wave rolls under you without breaking, but from its crest you can see three or four bigger waves stacking beyond it. The second wave is large enough to break, and you're in perfect position for it. You turn your specially modified single-fin around and begin stroking for your life to catch it. If you miss this wave, the ones behind it may very well drown you!

82

It's not long before a nice set comes in. Surprisingly, Nelly lets you take the first wave freely. You style into a spectacular barrel. The crowd on the beach gasps in awe as you pit yourself deep within the liquid vortex. Legendary surfers watch from the grandstand. And when you glide out from the bowl, they are smiling broadly.

Seconds later the air horn sounds, so you ride in on your belly. When you make it to the beach, you turn to look for Nelly and are relieved to see him paddling in from way outside—he didn't get a final wave.

You're now on the grandstand next to Nelly. Jacala Boy has long since been out of the contest, so when they announce Nelly as the second place winner, you know you've won. Bottles of champagne are poured over you. It's a sweet victory!

The End

The End

"Aaaah!" you scream as a giant, purple arm with suckers grabs you off your board and lifts you skyward. You look down and see the head of a monstrous octopus. Its silky black eyes stare at you like you're a lunchtime snack. You start punching at the rubbery arm that holds you tight. The great octopus lifts two more arms out of the water, each grabbing hold of one of your legs. You scream as it slowly pulls your legs apart. It keeps pulling until it has yanked one leg completely free from your body.

The octopus places your severed leg into its mouth. It disappears quickly. Then slowly, ever so slowly, you are forced foot first into its grinding maw.

To the amazement of Nelly, Jacala Boy, and everybody watching from the beach, you drop in on the first wave that comes. You're heading right towards the hapless water patrolmen on your ungainly board. The tube roars into shape and thunders down behind you, and it's a full-on obstacle course as you weave your way over and through the tangle of splashing and flipping watermen.

The barrel begins to break faster, so you crank a bottom turn to pull into the pit—but there's a lanky water patrolman and his board blocking your route. You decide to run over the hapless kook, aiming the nose of your board right over his rail.

b)

Heads - Page 117b   **Flip a coin**   **Tails - Page 126b**

a)

The currents become fast and wild, making it difficult to stay centered over your board. Giant swirls of chop edge up and drag you back and forth. You paddle with all your might to escape the fierce torrent but can't get any forward momentum.

You're moving in a large loop. The center of that loop is dropping out rapidly. You paddle for your life to escape the developing whirlpool, but it spins you round and round in a wide, vicious circle.

You hear an otherworldly sucking sound. In the center of the vortex, a funnel spins downward into the black depths. The vortex pulls at your feet and whips you around, trying to suck you in. You paddle with all your might, refusing to concede defeat in this tug-of-war with death. You try to make headway, but the whirlpool holds you fast.

84

You catch the frothy white wave and shoot to the bottom at high speed. The curl is breaking fast, so you immediately lean into a bottom turn—but Jacala Boy is floating right in your way! Jacala takes a breath and dives under. You feel your skegs bump something, but it's not enough to affect your balance. You hold your line and pull up into a spectacular tube. The wave spits at your back. You kick out to a rally of cheers from the beach.

The scoreboard lists high nines—you're stoked! You paddle back out to the lineup, amped to catch a few more waves.

"You dirty punk!" Jacala Boy yells. You turn and see the burly Hawaiian paddling towards you at full speed. A gash in his head is spilling blood over his face. He's a ways off. You look out to sea and spy a set marching in.

b)

a)

Two more heavy waves rumble by. Nelly does not resurface. You look to the horizon and see another set coming. You look back to the beach—the water patrol has not reacted yet. You make the decision instinctively—his life is at stake and you may be his last chance.

Nelly's board pops up a few meters away. You paddle over to it and pull up a broken leash. You undo your leash, take a deep breath, then dive into the depths.

You hold your breath for longer than you ever have. You find Nelly, grab his arm, and swim upwards with all your strength. You reach the surface and hear a roaring noise . . . the set from the horizon is unloading on you. You hold onto Nelly through the worst beatings you've taken in years. The whitewash carries you to the beach. Now the water patrol see you. They alert a group of medics, who come rushing over.

85

You smash directly into a tall coral head, grazing your knee and thrashing your thigh in the wipeout. The wave rolls over you and you emerge out the back of it.

Your board pops up next to you. About one foot of the nose has been smashed off completely. Angrily you climb back on your shortened board. Your leg hurts, but you're avoiding looking at it.

b)

a)

You get worked again. The whitewater tumbles you viciously about. When you finally resurface, you find your board is a single-fin. The side skegs have been broken off. You climb aboard and paddle towards the channel. You look back into the soup for any sign of Jacala Boy, but don't see him anywhere. You glance at your watch and realize the contest clock is ticking down. Someone on a Jet Ski is whipping around the inside looking for Jacala Boy, so you leave the rescue effort to them and paddle back outside.

You take your position beside Nelly, then glance towards the inside again. The person on the Jet Ski appears to be heading out further, and you still don't see Jacala Boy. You know you'll need another high-scoring wave in order to win this contest, so you cease to pay any attention to the rescue drama and focus instead on the horizon for signs of a set.

86

You launch off the lip and into a sick air. The board sticks to your feet as you sail into a smooth landing on the closeout wave.

While you are paddling back out, Nelly catches a bomb. He pulls into the tube in regular stance and exits it in switch stance. But he's not done! Riding switch stance he launches a 360 air.

You know you've been outdone by Nelly's sea-monkey performance. As you paddle back out to the lineup, you're cursing under your breath.

b)

a)

You're chest-deep in water. You feel the walls around you; they're craggy. There's an odor of dead fish. Then your hand touches something in the water that feels squishy and squirmy. Suddenly it moves!

You back away, but sharp prongs pierce into your neck. You grab the slimy thing that's attached itself to you and realize it must be a giant Moray Eel.

You stammer in agony and stumble around the darkened cave. But the harder you try to pull the tenacious creature from your neck, the deeper it burrows its teeth.

Your mind and body become strangely numb as the eel injects you with its paralyzing venom. You try to get away, crawling into a narrow tunnel.

87

You turn Jacala Boy over on his board and begin pushing him in. He's coughing and wheezing.

"That's it, Jacala Boy," you say, "just keep breathing, slow and steady."

He nods in affirmation. You look back and are thankful to see no more waves coming. Nelly is behind you. He offers to help, but you tell him not to worry. He reluctantly turns and paddles back towards the lineup. Moments later, the water patrol wade out and take Jacala Boy in on a water stretcher.

"Monitor his pulse and breathing," you tell them. "He blacked out. He's lost a lot of blood." You then take Jacala Boy's board—a beautiful gun—and paddle back out, lining up next to Nelly. A large set builds outside. You watch it longingly.

b)

The End

A strong undertow keeps you down, and with your equilibrium off kilter, you can only guess at which way is up. You can't hold your breath much longer. You immediately grab the leash at your ankle and give it a sharp tug. You look up and see your board tombstoning at the surface. You climb the leash hand over hand. But you don't get too far.

Your leash is yanking at your ankle, prohibiting upward progress. You look down and see it pulled tight. You try to swim harder, but you're unable to get any closer to the surface. You reach down and try to undo your leash, but the current is pulling so hard you can't reach your ankle strap. Your leash has snagged on a coral head. Tingle bells appear before your eyes. You drown.

"Nooooo!" you scream as you get sucked back over the falls. You feel momentarily weightless, then get slammed horrendously as the lip explodes into the flats.

As you are getting pummeled underwater, you open your eyes to see Nelly in the violent torrent of water just in front of you. The whirlpool is spinning him round and round like a rag doll nailed to a pinwheel. Suddenly you're sucked in and thrown at him at full speed! Your heads collide underwater and you are knocked out instantly. Your lungs fill with water and your heart stops.

The End

Heads - Page 102b   **Flip a coin**   **Tails - Page 110a**

a)

Paddle! Paddle! Paddle! You groan these words in your mind as you muscle your way through the strong currents and surging seas. You glance at your watch. There is still sufficient time to catch a bomb or two at Himalayas, an outer reef. You're paddling a sleek, long, spear-like surfboard—a true Hawaiian big-wave gun.

Great rollers rise up over the reef but do not break. Only forty-to-sixty-foot waves break this far out to sea. A massive set grows on the horizon. You calm your nerves and wait. Your heart beats so loud you can hear it as the wave comes. You're in perfect position. You turn and begin stroking down a six-story mountain of water.

89

A horde of medics closes in on you. You feel an injection; you feel them lifting you onto a stretcher. Your eyes become heavy; you are staring at the sun, then at the ceiling of an ambulance. The doors slam shut.

"Quickly!" a medic warns. "He's losing a lot of blood!"

You close your eyes and the blare of sirens turns into the noise of a carnival ride. You've slipped into a dream. Your parents are holding your hand. They look at you anxiously, worried about something. You look around and notice that everyone at the carnival is either a close friend or family member. Dark clouds take up the sky. A ferris wheel without lights rotates. The dream goes on and on. Will you ever wake up?

The End

The End

Your hand ends up in the one-eyed Hawaiian's mouth. He instantly bites down hard, severing two of your fingers and leaving a third dangling.

Jacala Boy starts to choke you, with both his hands clasped around your neck. The burly Hawaiian is dominating you, pushing you under the water. You should never have interfered with him in the first place. Regardless of who is to blame, you, my friend, are dead.

90

"Hey! Watch it!!" you scream as a burly woman on a Jet Ski races past you. She cuts a sharp turn, brings the ski to an idle and glides toward you. It's Tita Hulkington, the big-wave surfing legend.

"Grab the end of this," she says, tossing you a rope. "I'll get you into an Outer Logs bomb. We'll show the crowd what big waves are all about!"

She throttles the engine, lifting you out of the water in a snap. You're now standing on your board, holding the rope, and riding at twenty-five mph. Tita takes you far outside before turning back. A heavy roller grows beneath you. She's towing you into a humongous wave!

b)

Heads - Page 103b　　　**Flip a coin**　　　**Tails - Page 112a**

a)

With a sucking sound, the urchin is removed from your foot in one piece.

You're stoked to see that the urchin is still whole, but the pain coming from the bottom of your left foot is unbearable! You peer into the puncture marks. Your foot is entirely free from the infectious black spikes.

"Ow! Oow! Ooow!" you exclaim in pain. Your eyes water as you lie back on your board. You must fight through the pain. You're possibly one good ride away from the world title. You grit your teeth and paddle back outside.

As you take your position in the lineup, you keep a straight face, masking your pain from the others.

91

You jump with all your weight on to Jacala Boy, breaking his ribs with your knees.

The lifeguard picks you up and throws you headfirst into the sand, tweaking your neck severely. You sit up and try to straighten the kink out, but the lifeguard keeps up the aggression. He kicks you in the jaw and you feel your upper vertebrae snap. You lie there on the sand and can't feel a thing. You try to get up, but can't. Jacala Boy rolls on top of you and pushes your face into the sand. Pebbles clog your nose and stick to your lips. With every breath you take, you inhale more of the Pipeline beach. You try to cough, but you can't. Your muscles do not work from the neck down.

Those golden granules of Hawaiian sand which once held the promise of waves, sunshine, and victory, are now blocking your breath. You pass out as Jacala Boy sticks it to you. You are not revived.

The End

a)

Suddenly your board responds, and you pull up under the lip. The tube opens wide as you glide deep into it. You blast through the almond-shaped barrel, as it spits its fury at your back. To exit the wave you do a front-flip flyover. In the air you hear the judge's horn sound the end of the contest. You look at Nelly sitting on his board; he never caught a final wave.

"Eh brah!" Jacala Boy says to you on the beach. "Where you think you're goin?"

"I'm going up to the top step of the winner's podium to get my trophy," you respond. "Where you going?"

He becomes enraged, but by then a swarm of reporters have gathered around you. As the judges submit their tallies, you and Nelly go to center stage. JB hangs off to the side.

92

As you are taking a beating underwater, you bump into something and realize it can only be Jacala Boy Bones. You reach out and grab what feels like his arm. You hang on to it through the duration of your underwater pummeling.

At last you resurface, with Jacala Boy in tow. He appears unconscious. You swim him towards the beach. The water patrol soon comes to your assistance.

On the sand, the medics check his pulse and breathing before starting CPR. Members of his family gather around frantically. You try to console them.

Behind you, you hear a gurgle, then a watery cough. The audience erupts in cheers. Jacala Boy is back! His little daughter breaks through the cordon and flings herself into his arms.

b)

a)

You fall into the lip. It takes you down instantly. Your board shoots out towards Nelly.

You crouch on the reef for support, then eject up through the tumbling whitewater and break the surface. Unfortunately, your leash has snapped and your board is nowhere in sight. You are reluctant to swim in, but you have no choice.

On the beach, you find your board in three pieces! But it doesn't matter—the air horn sounds the end of the contest. You are out of luck. That was a terrible way to end a heat, you think. When you hear that Nelly got a bitchin' ride after your dramatic wipeout, your frustration peaks.

On the winner's platform, Jacala Boy takes third place and you get second. Nelly smiles as they place the giant $500,000 check in his hands. You leave the beach as the celebration begins. When you get to your jeep, you find the tires have been slashed and the windshield graffitied with surf wax: "Care of Da Hui and JB."

The End

a)

The water patrol and a team of medics work hard to revive Nelly.

Cough! Cough! Bulaaaat! Nelly comes a-vomiting back to life, spitting up loads of saltwater. The crowd cheers and his relatives rejoice. You're praised for wrestling him to shore.

But the jubilation for you has just begun. The judges tally the scores and you come out the winner of the Pipe Masters competition. As Nelly is helped to the stage to receive a second place trophy, he thanks you for saving his life. Champagne flows over your head as you're handed the trophy and a giant $500,000 faux check.

Just then Jacala Boy lumbers up to you and says: "Hey punk! I'm da real winner here! You're nuthin' but a cheatin' bastard! You're goin' down—now!"

94

The whale slams its broad tail down, crushing you. As the gargantuan mammal submerges below you, the undertow caused by its descent sucks you down with it.

With a fractured collarbone and both arms broken, all you can do is kick your feet for dear life. Slowly, ever too slowly, you make headway towards daylight.

On the beach the water patrol have been watching through binoculars. It's not long before they are speeding out to the rescue.

You're still kicking upward towards the surface. Bubbles float up as you expel your last breath. You hear the whale sounding and singing. You keep kicking. Any second now you're going to black out.

b)

a)

As Jacala Boy lies on a floating surfboard, coughing himself back to life, Nelly shamelessly paddles back out to keep competing. Greedy bastard! you say to yourself. But there's no denying he helped save JB.

You paddle Jacala Boy to the beach. Water patrolmen carry him up to the sand, where the medics go to work. His family gathers round, his mother hysterical and in tears.

"Don't worry, Mrs. Queenie Bones," you console her. "Jacala Boy is in good hands now. He's gonna be just fine."

She brushes away her tears, then crouches down to hold her son's hand. A few minutes later, he is taken off the oxygen and is talking coherently. He looks up at you with a glum smile as tears stream down the sides of his face, and says: "Mahalo nui loa, brah. You saved my life."

95

Your rail digs in deeper, throwing you off your board. You penetrate the wave face, but get carried up and over the falls. The ride is like being in a glass elevator, you can see through the wave to a blurry image of the shoreline and crowd. Then your world explodes. You come up dizzy. Your board has washed in, forcing you to swim the distance.

Just as you make it to the beach, the air horn sounds the official end of the contest. Nelly bagged two sweet waves during your hardships. You are ushered up to the grandstand and wait there beside Nelly. Jacala Boy, not surprisingly, is out of the contest. The announcement of Nelly as the winner puts you in second place. You were so close—only fractions below the champ! Nelly is handed the $500,000 giant check. That check would have been yours if you'd pulled the 360. You're awarded $75,000. It's the most unsatisfying money you've ever received. But there's always next year . . .

The End

a)

Commotion reigns as reporters, sponsors, and the contest announcers all come up with differing final scores. Meanwhile, Nelly continues to receive CPR, and the judges withhold the official scores until his situation is resolved.

Unfortunately Nelly is not revived. After twenty minutes of CPR, the medics throw in the towel, to tearful outbursts from his friends and family. Shortly thereafter, the judges somberly give the official results. You've won the Pipe Masters competition and are now the world's top surfer, but as the six-time former world champ lies there dead, you feel remorse rather than jubilation. You could have tried to help him, but you didn't.

"Coward!" Jacala Boy says, looking you square in the eyes. He clenches his fists. "It's your fault Nelly maki die dead!"

A lifeguard stands nearby, but he does not intervene as Jacala Boy swings at your jaw.

96

You're able to paddle into this wave. It's huge—about six stories tall. You're pushing the limits of paddle-in surfing, and the spectators and reporters on the beach can't believe what they are seeing. There, on Pipeline's outer reefs, you are a mere ant atop a mountain of water.

You plunge down to the trough and momentarily lose sight of the beach. This wave is so large that it is sucking fifteen feet or more below sea-level. You do your best to bottom turn, but it's useless—the wave is breaking too fast and there's too much water rushing up the face. You straighten out and trust to providence . . .

b)

a)

Every judge has given you a 10!

"Ooooh yeah!" you hoot, knowing your ride will go down in history as one of the most extraordinary moves ever pulled off at Backdoor Pipeline. You glance down at your watch and see there is less than a minute left in the heat. There are no more sets coming, leaving your rivals high and dry. You casually stroke towards shore.

Soon you and your opponents are standing on the winner's platform. Your final tally is higher than the others'—not by a huge margin, but it's a comfortable win nevertheless. There's great fanfare as champagne is poured over your head. Your Backdoor ride is played on the large video screen. Your opponents, and even Da Hui, want to shake your hand. Your barrel roll will become a legend.

97

You regain your balance just as Nelly loses his. You pull further up into the barrel and he falls into the lip. The cascading water takes him down like an ant getting slammed at the base of a waterfall. His board shoots up at you.

b)

The End

Your board remains unresponsive. The heaving Pipeline lip comes down squarely on your shoulders, blowing out your eardrums and breaking your neck. You get spun helplessly underwater like a rag doll in a washing machine. You are unable to swim towards the surface and soon run out of breath. You inhale saltwater and everything goes black. Your body is recovered, but you are not revived.

I'm sorry, my friend, but you are dead.

All is hysteria as the medics try to revive Nelly. For six of the longest minutes of your life, you hang your head low, and pray he'll pull through.

Suddenly Nelly coughs up saltwater and opens his eyes. He's been saved!

You and JB help Nelly up to the platform before a cheering audience. You stand beside him, helping to hold him up, while Jacala Boy takes his other side. JB takes third place, Nelly takes second place, and you're handed the winning faux check of $500,000. Jacala Boy turns to you with a smile and says: "Eh, brah. No hard feelings 'bout what happened in da water. You wus full on, ho you numba one!"

"Thanks," you say, patting him on the back, then you grab a full bottle of champagne and take a big swig. You've made it to the good life.

The End

a)

The pull on your ankle is strong as your board gets sucked over the falls, stretching your leash taut and dragging you towards disaster. You're slowly being dragged into the back of the wave. You're almost sucked into the falls, when suddenly your leash snaps, sparing you from disaster. The fate of your board, however, is anyone's guess. You begin swimming in to look for it. If you lose your board now, it's going to seriously set you back.

99

The judges announce the final scores, unaware that medics are attempting to revive Nelly. You're the contest winner and the new world surfing champion! You can't help smiling and raising your arms in the air, but you lose your smile when you see the medics giving up their effort to revive Nelly. He is dead, and you didn't do a thing to try to help him when he got in trouble in the water.

"I oughtta knock your lights out, punk!" Jacala Boy says. "You're no winner! What kind of winner turns a back on another person's life? You're a selfish coward, and da whole world will know it!"

You stutter, unable to respond. You have won the contest, but you will only ever be famous for letting Nelly drown.

The End

The End

"Ready to take a beating, brah?" Jacala Boy warns as he tugs on your leash, pulling you off your board.

"No, please!" you scream as you struggle to swim away.

You feel his brawny hands wrap around your neck. You reach up and grab his wrists, trying to force him off, but the burly Hawaiian sinks you underwater with his weight. He's not letting you up.

You're hoping he will let you up at the last second—just to teach you a lesson. But as that last second comes, a set wave lands on both of you. With no air left, you black out. You are dead. You are reincarnated as a brine shrimp—a favorite snack for sea turtles.

100 -

Jacala Boy grabs your leg and trips you. You fall to the sand. He is still gripping your leg, so you twist and land a hard punch on his forehead.

The lifeguard intervenes and breaks up the fight, but once you and JB get back to your feet, the lifeguard backs off and says, "Listen up! If you're gonna fight, fair's fair and you both have to be on your feet."

Jacala Boy staggers as he raises his fists. You show him yours in return and begin hopping about like a prizefighter.

He swings a right at your head. You deflect the punch. He throws a left at your jaw.

b)

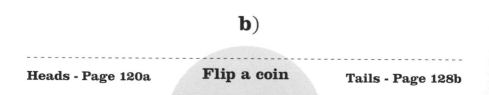

Heads - Page 120a   **Flip a coin**   **Tails - Page 128b**

Heads - Page 30b

Flip a coin

Tails - Page 124b

a)

Your head slams into a coral head, knocking you unconscious. The water pools red around you, alerting the water patrol to trouble. They hit the water and rush out to you.

Water spurts up from the rail of your board as you force it through the 360. From there you pull into a spectacular barrel, exiting amidst a spitting wind and fanfare from the beach. You look back to see your scores: 9.8, 9.9, 9.8, and a 10.

"Yeah!" you howl, knowing you deserve every fraction. You see Nelly on the outside, waiting for another set, so you begin stroking towards him, but then the air horn sounds the end of the heat.

The contest is over, and you've ended it on a solid ride. You're soon standing on the grandstand beside Nelly. Jacala Boy has long since been out of the contest. When Nelly is announced as the second place winner, you're showered with champagne—you've won the world title. Congratulations!

The End

a)

"Aaaaaah!" you scream in terror as the whirlpool sucks at your legs. You take a quick breath before you go under. Round and round you spin as you're drawn deeper down the descending column. You try to hold on to your board, but it slips from your grasp. You grow dizzy as the spinning gets faster. Then you're suddenly spun off to the side.

You swim upwards and surface quickly. You're surprised to find it's completely dark and the air smells mossy and damp. You've been sucked down deep and have ended up in an underwater cave! You reach out and feel a coral wall. You take deep breaths to calm your nerves. You're determined to survive this ordeal.

102

You're rising backwards up the face, gaining only slight forward momentum. When you're up at the lip, you're able to gain on physics. You quickly hop to your feet and drive down the wave—down some seventy-five feet.

Those watching you from the beach through binoculars cannot believe what they are witnessing. This is the biggest wave anyone has ever successfully paddled into. Even big-wave surfing legends watching from shore gasp in awe.

You bottom turn and the lip pitches over the deep reef. You are going inside the biggest tube ever ridden. The lip throws clean over your head. It sounds like an airplane engine inside, and it looks like a giant hangar with concave walls of blue glass. It's downright beautiful. Eventually the barrel shuts down and drowns you, but wow—what a way to go!

The End

a)

The wave rolls beneath you. You can't get into it. Your gut churns with fear. You turn to see the waves behind the one you missed and are struck with terror. An avalanche of whitewater is rushing at you.

Seconds before the flood hits, you take a deep breath and dive as deep as you can. The maelstrom hits you like a load of bricks and ruptures one of your eardrums, throwing your equilibrium out of whack. You fight to keep from tumbling head over heels, but it's useless. You're only wasting valuable energy, so you decide to let yourself be taken by the torrent. When you start running out of breath, you realize you might die.

103

As the massive peak grows and pitches, Tita Hulkington swings you deep into it. You let go of the rope and race down the face as she goes gunning for the shoulder. Before you know it, you're at the base of a wave some sixty-five feet high. The lip throws out, slotting you in the barrel of your life.

Tita hoots from the channel as you race out of the barrel then launch a huge air off the back of the wave—just for show.

"That was a shapely ride." Tita says over the rumble of her Jet Ski. Then she stands up, tightens her G-string, and says: "My turn now!"

b)

a)

The massive tail smacks down right next to you, throwing you off your board. You climb back on and the whale disappears.

A rogue wave marches in from the open sea. It peaks skyward over the Third Reef like a pyramid of water. You turn and stroke hard to catch it. The drop looks makeable, but the roller proves too big to paddle into. The wave rolls under you. Then, suddenly, you feel yourself being propelled forward! You're totally perplexed.

104

You get pummeled in the washing machine. While you're tumbling you can feel yourself bumping into Jacala Boy Bones. Finally the turbulence eases; you see daylight above and begin to swim towards the surface.

Before you make it to the top, you hear a bloodcurdling cry underwater. You look down and see the eyeless Jacala Boy swimming frantically below you. He reaches out and grabs your ankle.

You try to kick your leg free, but the burly Hawaiian just grabs your other ankle and holds on tight. He drags you down faster than you would've ever thought possible. He is totally out of breath and sinking fast.

You struggle again to break his grip on your ankles, but you can't. You look down. Jacala is bearing his teeth as he drags you into the depths.

The End

a)

You discover a large coral den with light reflecting up from a pool lined with silvery mollusks. But then you freeze. In the corner of this cave you see three decomposed bodies.

The corpses sport surf trunks. Are these people who went missing over the years, presumed drowned, their bodies never discovered?

Suddenly you hear a soft noise like a footstep of someone in the cavern, and a figure slowly emerges from a crevice. He is emaciated and pale, with a long beard, and he looks completely deranged. He comes towards you brandishing a surfboard skeg.

105

Another wave hits just before you reach the surface, knocking away the last of your air and driving you deeper. Your lungs are burning as you struggle in the maelstrom. Involuntarily, you take a big breath. Your lungs fill with water.

You go into coughing spasms as your lungs try to expel the saltwater. But each time you cough, you only take in more water. Soon your heart flip-flops in cardiac arrest.

Your mind drifts out of panic and into other thoughts: You could have been in Paris, hanging out with a friend you know there. You could have been in Australia, sharing a beer with some mates. You could have been surfing your home break. But noooo, you decided to fork out the cash to come to Oahu and try to win the Pipe Masters competition.

The End

a)

One by one, Jacala Boy's family and friends thank you for helping rescue him. You're also visited by a few of the judges, who thank you for your good sportsmanship and inform you that they've stopped the clock until you're ready to keep competing. Nelly is still sitting out the back, free surfing as the drama unfolds on land.

You look around for a board to ride, but your shaper is nowhere in sight. Fuming with rage, you yell out for him, but he can't be found.

Just then, legendary lifeguard Buck Quiggly hands you a strange-looking board and says: "Take it." It's experimental, looks almost alien, but you trust the glint in his eye.

"I'm going back out," you yell to the judges. You paddle out on Quiggly's board, and take your position beside Nelly. The air horn sounds to resume the contest.

106

You wait a long time for a wave to come. It's almost impossible not to show the pain you are feeling in your foot. You break a sweat in the water and your face turns red. Nelly looks at you curiously. You smile back at him but more strain than smile shows through.

"Constipation?" he asks. "No," you say, and leave it at that.

At last, a set spikes on the horizon. Jacala Boy snags the first wave. The second wave has a fat shoulder, so you and Nelly let it pass. The third wave is building nicely. You stroke, hop to your feet, and immediately serious pain shoots up your left leg. You drop down to a kneeling position and ride the bowl with both knees on the board. The air horn sounds the end of the contest before you finish the wave. The others soon come in and the scores are tallied. Jacala Boy wins, Nelly takes second, and you come in last. After all, this isn't a kneeboarding contest!

The End

The End

Reps from the top surf companies offer you contracts, throwing around words like millions, deal, once in a lifetime, and opportunity. You're too smart to accept any deal right off, but you take their business cards with the intention of setting up a bidding war later.

While you're giving lip service to Tita, your eye catches someone behind her. An attractive Brazilian bodyboarder is trying to get your attention. You leave big Tita in mid-sentence, and walk over to this alluring figure. What an amazing body! You share every moment of the next three weeks together. But the affair fizzles out when you get to know one another better. Hot body or not, you just totally annoy each other.

You've not seen each other in two months when one morning you hear a pounding at your North Shore door. It's the Brazilian bodyboarder's angry spouse. A gun is aimed at your head, and it's NOT a big-wave gun.

107

The three of you continue to exchange sneers and underhanded insults. After a tense wait, another set comes. You all let the first rollers pass, hoping for a slightly bigger and cleaner wave. But then you see an outside bomb that might clean you all up. The three of you spin around and start paddling for a medium-large wave—about twenty foot on the face.

This time, you're the deepest, Nelly is right beside you and Jacala Boy is scratching to hop on the shoulder. You stroke as hard as you can, then spring to your feet as the wave starts to jack.

"Ho! Ho!" you shout. "Comin' down!"

Nelly looks at you, but Jacala Boy pretends he doesn't hear you.

b)

Heads - Page 120b   **Flip a coin**   **Tails - Page 130b**

a)

As you crawl deeper into the narrow tunnel, the eel grates against the coral walls and releases its grip on your neck.

You finger the two deep punctures on your neck. You're in a daze. You shiver, and this leads into muscle spasms, then projectile vomiting. The eel's venom is putting you in a living hell. Mercifully you pass out.

You awake. You don't know how much time has passed. You don't feel great, but it looks like you've survived the eel attack. You crawl out of the crevice and make it back to the main cavern. Gingerly, you feel your way through the room and come to what feels like a corner. You round it and feel a rush of hope.

108

The first few waves break more towards Backdoor, prohibiting you and Nelly easy access. In the meantime, Jacala Boy is just about upon you.

"Eh brah!" he shouts. "You gonna get punished now!"

His expression is one of crazy vengeance. Blood is dripping from the side of his head as he paddles full speed at you.

A wave shifts your way, so you stroke hard to get into it—but so do Nelly and JB. As the peak jacks and you spring to your feet, Nelly backs off, but Jacala Boy goes. You try to ignore him and focus on the drop. It's steep, but you make it. Problem is, Jacala Boy has made it too, and as you both bottom turn up into the barrel, he looks at you with the worst of intentions.

b)

The End

Paddle! Paddle! Paddle! you scream in your mind. You're making no headway, but you don't give up. Eventually, you are spinning slower and in a wider arc. You redouble your efforts and are soon paddling in a relatively straight line. You've broken free! You see a set unloading on the outside reef known as Himalayas, so you immediately set your line towards that.

Some ten minutes later, you're lining up as best you can on the outside peak. A wave grows on the horizon like a blue volcano taking shape. It feels like an eternity before it's upon you. You spin around and paddle for it, giving it all you've got. You catch it, make the drop, then pull up into a barrel that could swallow an entire apartment complex. You make it out, then ride towards shore. Minutes later, you're on the beach at Pipeline, claiming the world title!

109

You hear an explosion. Another wave hits just before you reach the surface, driving you back down into the depths and spinning you like a rag doll in a washing machine. You're totally out of breath, so you give up fighting and go into Zen mode. Soon, an upwelling brings you to the surface.

Your equilibrium is tweaked, your leash is snapped, and you can't find your board. Two more waves hit you from behind. Eventually, you crawl up onto the beach. You lay on your back, breathing hard. Medics come to your aid.

"I'm okay," you pant. You rest for a moment, and regain your wits. Johnny Daring, legendary 1970s Pipeline surfer, approaches you carrying a board that has the word Pipecleaner stenciled on it. "There's still time to catch another wave," he says, handing you the board. You thank him humbly, then paddle back out and sit beside Nelly.

b)

Heads - Page 82b   **Flip a coin**   **Tails - Page 146a**

a)

You're able to get in and make the drop—an incredible feat on a wave of this magnitude. But when you go to crank a bottom turn, your board is unresponsive. You aren't used to this stick, and the wave is moving too fast to allow you to bottom turn. You straighten out and lean forward to generate as much speed as possible, as the super heavy breaker lunges at your heels. Will you get mopped up by the whitewater behind you?

110

It feels like an eternity, but another set eventually comes. Your foot is throbbing horribly and you wonder if you'll even be able to stand on your board.

Nelly nabs the first wave of the set, but in a rare moment for the pro, the bottom drops out and he freefalls into the pit, wiping out and scoring nothing.

You and Jacala Boy let the second and third waves pass. The fourth is a monster and Jacala is too deep for it. You race for the shoulder, stroking for your life to get into it. You're caught up in the lip for a second, but soon go lunging down into the trough. You attempt a bottom turn, but sharp pains shoot from your foot up your leg.

The lip begins to fall swiftly down. You must turn up and into the barrel now or you will get hit by the lip—"axed," as they say on the North Shore. You grit your teeth and initiate the turn . . .

b)

a)

There, in a roomy coral den, are piles of gold medallions, silver coins, and gemstones! A faint light comes through a distant wall.

You walk around what must be millions of dollars worth of booty. Open chests overflow with pearls and . . . human bones. You peer down at the side of the chest and can make out in the flickering light: H.M.S. Yamamoto. The room you're in looks square—too square, in fact, to be a natural cavern. You walk up to one of the walls and tear away a loose clump of coral, and find steel. You've been pounded into the hull of a sunken vessel! You look around at the spoils and dollar signs light up in your eyes. You want to take some of this treasure back up with you—all of it, in fact—but this is not possible at present. You have to devise another plan.

111

You pass out and dream that you are at an amusement park. You're a child. It's crowded. People are walking all around you. All that you can see are legs. Legs, legs, everywhere. You look up for your mother. But you are lost, alone and scared.

The next thing you know, you wake up in a hospital bed. You throw your bed cover aside and almost vomit at the sight: one of your legs has been amputated. It is bandaged at the femur.

Your manager is in the room beside you. "My leg . . . Did I win?" you ask.

"Nelly won," says your quirky manager. "Yer doc said he had ta take off yer leg, but with modern prosthetics you'll be da bionic surfer!"

You start crying.

The End

a)

Tita whips you into a massive wall, then speeds off the back. You carve down the face, taking wobbly swoops from side to side in the style of Mavericks surfer, Gwen "Goonybird" Burnham. You set up for the bowl, then race as fast as you can into a gaping barrel.

You see Tita again, on the wave's shoulder, trying to hoot you on. This is the biggest barrel she's ever seen anyone ride. Giant drops of water begin to fall in front of you, ten gallons apiece. The tube is beginning to close.

"Race ahead! Race ahead!" she screams.

More giant droplets fall, just missing you. You do as Tita says and jet towards daylight. But the once-open exit is quickly turning into a great chandelier of falling water. You brace yourself for the onslaught, hoping to plow through the corrupted end section.

112

You happily hold your giant faux check of $500,000. You're offered various multi-million-dollar deals on the spot, but you are most attracted to one mainstay sponsor who offers you a five-year contract, which they say they will honor even if you decide to stop competing.

Beyond the noise and activity of the festivities, you see the general surfing public paddling out at Pipeline once again. The contest is officially over, so the wave is given back to the North Shore to share or fight over. You watch a series of sets comb the outer reefs, then barrel across the Pipeline reef. You want to paddle back out, but are being pressured by interviewers. You start to realize that you don't want to be trapped in rigid contest schedules and circuits, you don't want to have to attend endless board meetings and functions. You want more freedom!

b)

The End

The giant eel drags you back from the narrow tunnel and into its den. It places you on a reef ledge, then releases its grip. Your body is now completely immobilized by the paralyzing venom.

Suddenly, your ankles are snagged by something sharp. You barely have any sensation left in your body, but you feel a suction at your feet. The suction feeling moves slowly up your body. You are being swallowed alive!

You scream your last scream, as the mouth of the eel pulls your head in. Your world goes black as tusk-like fangs sink into your eyes. In a final gulp, you disappear. Abra cadaver.

A seemingly endless throng of Jacala Boy's friends and family members come to thank you for helping save his life.

"You da hero of da day," his father says to you teary-eyed. "I want to invite you into Da Hui. Da boyz will make sure you get any wave you want on da North Shore. Thank you. Aloha!"

You feel humbled by this formal initiation into the ranks of the North Shore local crew, but more so by the tears of joy in the eyes of old Wiley Bones.

Just then, the air horn blasts the formal end of the heat. You had long since forgotten the contest was underway! In that time Nelly bagged a series of rides. He arrives on the beach and marches up to the grandstand. You're requested to join him there, while Jacala Boy stays with the medics. When the scores are announced, Nelly wins, but you're the hero of this year's Pipe competition.

The End

- -

a)

Suddenly your board pops up out of the water. It's still in one piece, but just three feet of leash remains attached to the leash plug. You'd just as soon surf the rest of the contest without a leash, but decide to take a few seconds to reconnect it anyway. It seems easier than undoing it from your board and ankle. You tie the two ends together into a strange but effective knot, then paddle back out towards the lineup.

Nelly and Jacala Boy are paddling back out as well. Jacala Boy got a decent score from his ride. He is getting the edge on you now. You get situated next to your rivals and resolve to practice better wave selection.

114

- -

A split second after the photographer takes your picture, you collide with his camera housing, smashing his face as you go flying over the nose of your board. You dive into the wave's trough and it rolls over you without further incident. The cameraman, however, gets caught inside. He resurfaces moaning in pain.

Water patrol members are also caught inside, dealing with problems of their own. As more waves keep unloading, you duck-dive your big board, leaving the luckless photographer and the water patrol to their own devices. You glance back and see your score. The highest is a measly 5.1. You curse the cameraman for ruining your perfect ride.

Once you're outside, the air horn sounds the end of the contest. You scream in frustration, then paddle all the way to the beach and throw your hulky board angrily onto the sand. Your opponents are already on the grandstand. You join them, as anger floods through you.

b)

- -

a)

You see Nelly take off on a perfect wave that should have been yours if JB hadn't forced you out of position. The threatening Hawaiian continues to paddle towards you at full speed.

Another peak jacks up in front of you. You're too deep, but you go for it rather than face the inevitable wrath of JB.

When Jacala Boy sees you trying to escape, he paddles and tries to drop in on you. You rocket to the bottom of the wave and see him caught in the lip. There's no way he'll make the drop, but he seems intent on taking you out.

You widen the arc of your bottom turn as much as possible to avoid his falling path, but you must keep your turn tight enough to pull into the massive barrel now taking shape. If you do this right, he'll be thrown over the falls and get utterly worked while you'll race clean through the cavern and score big.

115

A set rises over the outer reefs. Nelly is determined to keep you from scoring another good wave. He paddles hard to get deeper. You're frustrated that he's claiming your spot. You paddle harder than him, towards Backdoor. You easily glide ahead of him while Jacala Boy stays put and focuses intensely on the horizon.

The first wave builds into a perfect left. You're deep, too far out of position, but you try for the wave anyhow. You paddle with all your might to get into it early. Nelly pulls back.

The wave is legitimately yours, and you ride it with full-on speed and in a relaxed style. After riding through a spectacular tube, you perform a Bertlemann carve at the barrel exit.

b)

a)

"I'm going down?" you respond to Jacala Boy's threats.

"Yeah, dat's right, punk!" he snarls back, then lumbers up to you and swings at your head. You duck, then immediately strike a hard upper cut to his chin, rendering him unconscious. You shake your fist out as he lies there on the sand. Suddenly, out of nowhere, a group of heavy Hawaiian local boyz surrounds you.

"Eh brah," the biggest of the bunch says as he saunters up to you with clenched fists, "how's dat false crack? You just put one of our braddahs down, and to put one of our ohana down is to put us all down."

At first you are frightened, but you hold your ground and respond: "He came at me first, and I won the fight fair and square."

116

You're on the verge of blacking out. Tingle bells appear before your eyes. At last, you reach the surface and take a deep breath, warding off death! The water patrol is coming on a Jet Ski, and you're totally relieved to see them.

Suddenly, the seventy-foot whale surfaces right beside you. You stare into its large, steady eye, before it submerges again. You swim hard to keep out of the creature's self-made undertow.

Seconds later, the Jet Ski arrives and a water patrolman reaches down and hoists you onto the safety sled. He gets ready to throttle the engine, then all of a sudden the great whale resurfaces again! The Jet Ski rises up on its back and you fall into the sea. The whale smacks its tail all around, hitting you both numerous times. Ultimately the two of you drown. When Jacala Boy gets wind of the tragedy, he is angered at how you carelessly imperiled others.

The End

The End

A huge spout of water shoots up right next to you. The whale is directly beneath you. Now it is lifting you slightly upon its back, just above the water's surface. Faster and faster it swims, catching up with the giant wave that had passed you.

As the whale submerges, your board connects with the water and you pop up to your feet. The whale peels off the backside as you carve up and down the face of this massive wave. You pull into a hotel-sized barrel, ride through it, then exit with your arms raised in victory.

Onshore, people are confused about how you caught a wave that had passed you. You keep your secret as you accept the winner's trophy, promising to yourself that you will become a whale activist. As for Jacala Boy—he is disqualified for poor sportsmanship.

You run squarely into the water patrolman's board; your skeg cuts through his rail. You go flying off your board and get hammered by the wave. When you come up for air, your board is broken in three, and several of your pursuers surround you.

"You're going to the beach!" a burly water patrolman shouts, then swims towards you. He reaches a brawny arm around your shoulder and begins swimming you in. You are locked in place by his muscular arm, with a close-up view of the sailor's anchor tattoo on his bicep.

"Let go of me, kook!" you demand of the lantern-jawed hunk.

He forces your lips to his and says with a false lisp: "You're all mine, sweetie."

The End

a)

Tita Hulkington dives off the Jet Ski as you take her place behind the handlebars. She finds the end of the tow rope and gives you the pinky-up signal. You throttle the PWC, lifting her out of the water as she rides upon your recently acquired big-wave surfboard.

"Go! Go! Oh please, go!" she shouts fervently, pointing her pinky at a giant set a few hundred yards out.

You gun the Jet Ski at full-throttle, then make a wide, elliptical turn into the fifth roller, whipping Tita into it. She releases the rope and flings down into the pit. She stalls at the base of the wave, letting it grow larger. As the big lip throws, she leans a bottom turn into one of the hugest barrels you've ever seen! You're mesmerized.

You look ahead of you and realize you have ridden to the base of the jacking wave! You turn and aim up towards the pitching lip, hoping to punch through it and emerge safely out the back.

118

Jacala Boy is so intent on catching you that he's no longer watching the falling lip of the wave. It comes down, nipping his outside shoulder and dragging him under.

You fade deeper and deeper into the barrel until your whole world is blue. Sunlight bends in through the walls of the wave and a giant snowball rolls at your back. It's a moment you will never forget. You pump your board a few times and get a shot of speed that sends you rocketing out the barrel exit. You throw your fists up triumphantly just as the air horn sounds to close the contest. The crowd erupts in cheers. You score four 10s, and that seals your win!

The End

The End

"Please!" you cry aloud as the pain in your stump gets worse. "Please, put me under!"

The medic beside you says, "Here, take some of this." He injects some morphine into your butt cheek. It burns as it goes in.

The ambulance comes to a screeching halt, and you're rushed into the hospital and wheeled beneath an operating lamp. A white-masked surgeon stands over you with a large needle. "Where's the leg?" he asks his assistants.

You wake up a long time later and look down at your legs. They are both there. You try to wiggle your toes on your once-severed leg. They only twitch!

"You might be surfing again . . . some day," your nurse says with an ambiguous smile. "But you ought to take up bird watching instead. By the way, that contest you were surfing in—it was called off."

Your foot can't handle the bottom turn—the pain is so intense that your leg buckles. You fall into the pit and quickly get sucked out the back of the wave. You resurface to find your board broken in three, forcing you to swim to shore.

As you backstroke in, you see both Nelly and Jacala Boy take off on bombs and pull into spitting barrels. The spectators lining the beach cheer wildly.

Just as you crawl onto the beach, the air horn sounds the end of the contest. Medics carry you further up the beach. You feel humiliated by all the extra attention.

After Nelly and Jacala Boy come ashore and the scores are tallied, your humiliation deepens. Jacala Boy wins first place, Nelly takes second and you place third, which is last.

The End

The End

Jacala Boy's punch connects and your teeth go flying. "Locals only, brah! Go home," he says.

You look up into a series of microphones and cameras and say nonchalantly as you wipe the blood from your chin, "In my honest assessment, I think I should have gotten first place, and Jacala Boy should have been disqualified for unsportsmanlike conduct."

The reporters look at you perplexed. Your words are slurred and unrecognizable, because you're talking through broken teeth. Neither the judges, reporters, nor contest sponsors will admit that the contest has become a mockery. You complain bitterly to your manager. He responds with three words: "Get over it."

120

- -

At the last second Nelly pulls back, but Jacala Boy blatantly drops in on you. As you race to the pit and crank a bottom turn, he rockets down just in front of you, missing you by a hair's breadth. Thing is, you've pulled right up into the barrel and the lip is falling far ahead, meaning Jacala Boy will get shut out.

But the pressure is not off—you're far back in a hard-breaking cylinder and it's going through multiple internal spits, repeatedly blasting compressed air and mist through the tunnel. One shot of air is so strong that it causes to you teeter forward. You're losing your balance.

b)

Heads - Page 64b   **Flip a coin**   **Tails - Page 69a**

The End

"And the winner is . . ." You hold your breath as the loudspeakers blare your name. The crowd erupts in cheers as bottles of champagne are uncorked. Sweet victory at last! Nelly comes in second, while Jacala Boy takes third. Surprisingly, nobody has been disqualified.

Suddenly an empty champagne bottle hits the back of your head, knocking you unconscious. You awaken on a stretcher, being carried towards an ambulance, a huge throbbing lump on your head. Reporters crowd around.

"Patient has suffered a concussion," a medic is saying into his radio, "and will need stitches."

You look over and see a handcuffed Jacala Boy being put into the back of a police car. You never imagined winning the world title would be like this.

You're so excited from your ride that you're torn between paddling right back out to nab another one and stopping to look back for your scores. You end up paddling back out to the lineup, glancing behind you every few seconds, waiting to see the results.

Your rivals look alternately from you to the beach to the outside, not happy that the clock is running down when you've just caught a nice wave.

b)

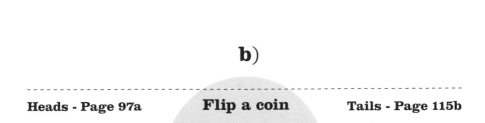

Heads - Page 97a   **Flip a coin**   **Tails - Page 115b**

a)

Snap! Snap! Snap! Snap! Snap! The cameraman fires off a sequence of shots as you race by him. As you exit the tube and cut back on the shoulder, the air horn sounds the end of the contest. You jump to your belly and let the bucking whitewater glide you to the sand. Your scores are raised—one is a 10! The water patrol swim or get washed in behind you. They are yelling, but you ignore them. As far as you're concerned, you did nothing wrong. In fact, you think the crowd views you as the surfing hero of the contest.

Jacala Boy, Nelly, and the cameraman all make it to the beach. You mount the grandstand beside your competitors and wait for the winner to be announced.

122

"Fair fight, eh?" asks a large Samoan, as the other local heavies look at you.

"Sure was," you respond. "One-on-one, no weapons. Besides, Jacala Boy is bigger than me—much bigger."

They look at you and then at their defamed comrade lying in the sand. The big Samoan, who appears to be the leader, takes the rest a few paces away, where they form a huddle. Your knees practically tremble at what's going to happen next. These boyz could beat you so badly it might end your surfing career.

The gang breaks from their huddle. They slowly surround you, their burly arms crossed over their wide chests and bulging stomachs. The large Samoan points his finger in your face and says: "Eh brah! You must be one mean dog to beat Jacala Boy, so we've decided to let you into our tribe. Welcome to Da Hui. Hang loose, brah."

The End

a)

Your plan is, first, to get out of this sunken treasure trove, then to return later with a crew to retrieve the spoils. You make your way to where the reflected light is shining. You trace the reflection to a hole in the floor, where a pool of abalone-type mussels cling to the bottom. Their silvery backs reflect sunshine from an exit somewhere off to the side.

Before you dive in, you look down and notice a large necklace. Its chain is pure gold and it carries a diamond almost the size of a baseball. The jewel glistens in the reflected light. You pick it up. It's heavier than it looks. You fasten the necklace around your neck, take a deep breath, then dive into the glowing pool.

123

Your board just misses Nelly's head. A second later you get pummeled fiercely by the cascading lip. The water holds you under for quite some time, weighing on you like liquid cement. Meanwhile, on the surface, Nelly makes his ride and scores big.

After getting washed far inside, you carefully step down on to the coral to stop your drift.

b)

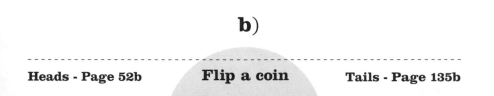

The End

You open the throttle on the Jet Ski. You're at full power, but you still don't make it over the pitching lip in time. You go over the falls upside down while seated on the heavy craft. You hear an angry holler from below.

"Look out!" Tita roars.

You're thrown over her, and you break your collarbone when you land. But at least the Jet Ski didn't hit you or Tita. She calls to you from the channel. Against all odds, she made the wave. Another breaker unloads on your head, driving you painfully into the depths. You're underwater for a long time. You take twenty strokes towards the surface, but it's still distant. You look up and see Tita paddling around on the surface. You reach up and exhale the last of your air. It rises towards the surface in so many swirling bubbles.

124

A water patrolman reaches you and swims you to the beach. The side of your head is throbbing painfully. You'll need many stitches.

As you're led to a waiting ambulance, the air horn sounds the official end of the contest. You convince the medics to allow you to hear the contest results before they drive you to the hospital.

To your dismay, Nelly is announced as the winner; you come in second. But you're happy to hear that Jacala Boy has been disqualified.

You're loaded into the ambulance and driven to a hospital on the east side of the island.

b)

Heads - Page 144a   Flip a coin   **Tails - Page 148a**

The End

Nelly's board just misses you as it—along with Nelly—is hurled into an oblivion of exploding whitewater. You focus your attention on making the barrel. Time seems to slow down as the lip throws widely over you.

You exit the tube and hear the crowd on the beach erupt in cheers. The air horn sounds the end of the contest as your scores are raised. A 9.6, 9.5 and two 9.8s! Not bad, considering you could have been called for interference. Either it was called on Nelly, or the judges deemed you made the wave fair and square. As for Nelly, he gets washed in a few minutes later.

You step up to the grandstand. Both Nelly and Jacala have angry words for you. When the scores are announced, you're drenched with champagne! Jacala Boy comes in last, Nelly second, and you first. You win!

You burst through the cascading water into bright sunlight. The lip closes down behind you a split second later. You made it!

You let out a howl of joy as you go flying off the back of the wave.

"That was phat . . . real phat," Tita Hulkington says as she picks you up. "You might win the contest with that ride."

"The contest!" you exclaim. You had forgotten completely about it. You look down at your watch and see the seconds counting down: three – two – one. Just then, you faintly hear the air horn sound the official end. Your wave counted!

b)

Heads - Page 142b   **Flip a coin**   **Tails - Page 151a**

The End

As the lip throws, you gun the Jet Ski towards the top of the wave, aiming to break through it, but the lip catches you and throws you out and over Tita some sixty feet below.

"Hey!" is the last thing you hear Tita say as you and the Jet Ski slam down directly on her.

You're pummeled mercilessly, as if the wave is trying to rip your arms and legs off. You resurface dazed but unharmed. The Jet Ski is nowhere in sight. What's worse, Tita is also nowhere to be found. You search for her as best you can in the frothy aftermath, but to no avail.

You eventually have to admit to the terrible fact that Tita was killed in the accident. The water patrol come out and rescue you. Arriving on the beach without Tita is sad. You don't even care that you've been disqualified from the contest as a result of Jacala Boy Bones' protests.

126

You plow right over the water patrolman's board without losing your balance. You have just enough momentum to pull under the lip.

You get closer to the face and are rewarded with a sudden rush of speed that sends you through a blue tube and then out into the daylight!

The crowd erupts in rapturous cheers!

b)

Heads - Page 121b   Flip a coin   **Tails - Page 133b**

The End

Your board rides like a dream. It's responsive, fast, and accelerates out of turns. You glide out into the sunshine and start carving up a wall with style. A broad wake fans out from your high rail as the air horn sounds the end of the heat.

Hoards of admirers flock around you on the beach and praise your style.

You mount the grandstand beside your opponents. Jacala Boy is announced as the third place winner. He shakes his head, then steps back for the next announcement.

"And the winner of the Pipe Masters event is . . . Nelly Yater!"

Underwater, you hear the sound of a humming engine, then you black out.

"He's back!" a water patrolman shouts as you regain consciousness. You're lying on the back seat of a Jet Ski, coughing up salty spume.

On the beach, there's a flurry of concern and jubilation as you're helped up to the grandstand. You stand beside your opponents. You're dizzy and water drips from your nose. Nelly takes first place. You take second. You lean over to Jacala Boy and say, "My board rode great, Mr. Bones. Mahalo."

The End

The End

You round the corner. In the center of a large coral den, a steady light undulates from deep within a pool lined with silvery mollusks. In the pool there's a three-foot-wide crevice through which the light spills in.

Seeing a way out gives you renewed energy. Without further ado, you take a deep breath, hope there are no more eels lurking about, and plunge into the glowing water. You swim through the crevice towards the light.

It becomes difficult to hold your breath, but you reach the end of the crevice and look up to see the ocean surface not far off. Suddenly the giant eel snags your leg and draws you back into its lair.

128 -

You dodge out of the way and Jacala Boy's punch misses. You fire back, landing a strong punch on his temple. He falls back to the sand, unconscious.

As you shake your fist out, some in the crowd clap while others curse you in Pidgin, a Hawaiian slang. A group of hulking local ruffians approaches you.

"Eh brah!" a massive man with missing teeth and a Samoan build says as he lumbers up to you. "We Da Hui North Shore Crew, and you just punched out our little bruddah."

You look up at him steely-eyed, but the man is humongous, and your expression turns to fear. He has a series of Maori-style tattoos across his arms, chest and neck, and "LOLO" tattooed across his forehead.

"Yeah, that's right," you respond coolly. "It was a fair fight, and he went down."

b)

Heads - Page 122b   Flip a coin   **Tails - Page 138b**

The End

You quickly close a deal with the sponsor offering the five-year "free surfing" contract, the one where you won't have to compete relentlessly in order to get paid. Almost immediately after signing the contract, his assistants bring some boards down to the beach.

"Those look nice," you say. "Here, give me that yellow board—the surf's still cranking!"

You're handed the stick and jostle through the crowds back towards the water. The media is stunned by your actions. Your left foot hurts from the previous round—you tweaked it a bit—but you're feeling good enough to keep surfing.

After the contest you travel the world, shunning the professional circuit and the limelight, riding perfect waves where you can find them. Eventually you settle down at Cloud 9 in the Philippines. You marry and have kids. Your kids want to become pro surfers, but you send them to college instead.

"Food!" moans the crazy, emaciated guy as he comes towards you with the surfboard skeg. Then he lunges at you.

You jump sideways and he goes tumbling to the floor. You hustle over to the pool of shining mollusks, take a deep breath, and dive in.

You follow the light that's causing the shells to reflect so brilliantly. There's a narrow opening along a submerged coral wall. You swim towards it, believing you'll be able to squeeze through and reach the sunlight above.

You hear a splash underwater and turn to see the lunatic swimming after you, the surfboard skeg held squarely between his teeth. You begin swimming faster towards the light, but he's gaining on you quickly!

b)

Heads - Page 138a   **Flip a coin**   **Tails - Page 152a**

The End

"What?" you respond to Jacala Boy. He marches up to you and socks you hard in the jaw before you even have a chance to react. You fall to the sand with a bloody mouth.

"That teaches you to come ova here and act like you can do anything!" says Jacala. He rears back to kick you, but he's seized from behind by a group of lifeguards.

As you get up and wipe the blood from your mouth, two policemen approach and handcuff Jacala Boy. Then, to everyone's amazement, Nelly, as if back from the dead, saunters up to Jacala Boy and spits in his face.

"I love Hawaii," Nelly tells him, "and I respect Hawaiians. But I hate sore losers."

130

As you are dropping in, so is Nelly. Jacala Boy backs out at the last second.

You bottom turn and Nelly rockets down in your path. You pull up into a hard- and fast-breaking barrel, and Nelly gets shut out. Your board surprises you by garnering speed of its own, rapidly driving you towards the closing gap. You race out of the tube and throw your fists up in glory. Just as you kick over the back of the wave, you hear the air horn sound the end of the contest.

Nelly incurs an interference call on the last wave, costing him the contest— he comes in third. Congratulations! You win!

The End

a)

As Tita dives off the Jet Ski, you reluctantly take the handlebars. This is not what you wanted—you're still in a contest and still have time to score another bomb, but now Tita wants to get a wave, too.

She flashes you the pinky-up signal. You throttle the engine, and she springs up out of the water. You look back and she points her pinky outside where a big set is building. You drive into the first wave and whip her around. She lets go of the rope and glides down into the pit. She stalls her bottom turn, adjusts her G-string, then leans sharply into a gaping barrel. You hoot her on, then turn to throttle over the wave.

To your horror, the lip is already pitching in front of you. You're trapped!

You look back to see a large bull shark biting into the tail of your board. It's thrashing and pushing you forward.

You grip your board with white knuckles. The shark's jaws are less than twelve inches from your feet. You lift your legs as it continues chomping up the back of your board.

You take desperate paddle strokes to put distance between you and this beast. But the shark has the bottom three feet of your battered board in its mouth and is swimming right behind you.

You decide you'd be better off jettisoning your board and swimming for shore. Perhaps the shark will continue to chew on your board and leave you alone. Just before you roll off the side, the shark lurches forward and crushes both your legs in its jaws. The water turns red as you emit an involuntary groan.

The End

The End

Your board rides superbly and so do you, as you glide out into the afternoon sunlight. Johnny Daring, 1970s Pipeline demigod, admires your ride from the jacuzzi of a beachfront home.

Just after you exit the barrel, you hear the air horn sound the end of the contest. Perfect! you scream inside. You angle your hefty board in towards shore. As you jump to your belly, your board catches some big chop and flips over. You land crotch–first on the large skeg.

"Ouuuuuuuu!" you wail in pain as you struggle to free yourself.

Soon you're standing on the podium, one hand clutching your bleeding crotch and the other holding the giant $500,000 check. You've won, but you're embarrassed and headed to the emergency room.

- -

The tip of Nelly's board shoots into your eyeball. You fall from your board and get held under. You resurface on the inside, holding a hand over your eye and moaning like a dying cow. Nelly resurfaces right next to you and says, "That's what you get for interfering with my ride, kook!"

The air horn blasts, ending the contest. Nelly swims towards shore. You do your best to swim in, but make little progress. The water patrol come out and help you in.

On shore, medics surround you in a panic because your eyeball has fallen out and is hanging by the nerves. Jacala Boy is held back by two lifeguards as he screams about how he will get you when you least expect it. Then the announcers say that Jacala has won the contest, and Nelly has been disqualified for unsportsmanlike behavior. It cost you an eye to win second place.

The End

The End

You proceed to the pool containing the glittering mollusks, dive in, and swim towards the light. You find a crack in the wall and follow it, then eject up to the ocean surface.

Water patrolmen are buzzing around on Jet Skis, and they soon find you.

Not surprisingly, you lose the Pipe Masters contest, but everyone is interested in hearing your story. You tell them you were awash in high seas and that's why they couldn't see you from the beach. You don't mention the cave or the treasure. Jacala threatens to pounce on you for interfering with him. You apologize as humbly as you can, but inside you laugh, because you know that soon you'll be rich!

Six days later you and two friends scuba dive and recover the precious stones, gold, and silver. You're set for life!

133

You look back at your score and see all high numbers—including two 10s! You're stoked that you mastered the ungainly board. Soon the air horn sounds the official end of the heat.

Your board paddles fast, so you arrive on the beach before your competitors. You watch as some water patrolmen climb onto the beach, exhausted. "Idiots," you say under your breath. One water patrolman hears it, and gets in your face, claiming you endangered his whole crew. You just laugh and walk to the grandstand.

Jacala is announced as the second place winner. He backs off, then you're announced as the first place winner. There's a roar of cheers. All respect the outcome—even Nelly, who comes in last.

The End

The End

Jacala Boy is announced as the second place winner. He bows stoically to the audience, then sneers at you.

"And the first place winner of the Pipe Masters event, who will take home the world title, is . . ." You close your eyes, clench your fists, tilt your head up and hold your breath. "Nelly Yater!" With that announcement, you lower your head in defeat as the crowd erupts for Nelly.

A contest judge approaches you. "So I came in last, eh?" you ask with a tinge of disgust.

"Actually," he says diplomatically, "I've come to tell you that you didn't place at all. You were disqualified for unsportsmanlike behavior and fined $5,000 by the association."

134

- -

Jacala Boy gets thrown clean over you as you pull into a gaping barrel. It's surreal—a bleeding and screaming man caught in the crystalline lip—like something from a strange painting.

The barrel is so perfectly hollow that it is, in 1970s Pipeline surfer Johnny Daring's words, a "bowel drainer." Time seems to slow down as the massive cylinder rotates around you.

You make it out and then whip three sharp carves off the shoulder. The crowd goes berserk, and the judges are fairly impressed. Your scores are raised, and soon the air horn sounds the end of the heat. Your ride garnered some high nines. You only hope your overall score will shut out your competitors.

b)

Heads - Page 140b   **Flip a coin**   **Tails - Page 150a**

a)

Your board hits Nelly's chest hard and he goes down.

The powerful breaker pummels you both severely. You surface totally out of breath, but are fortunate that your board is floating near you and is still in one piece. You clamber onto it and quickly paddle towards the channel as more waves continue to explode over the shallow reef.

Once in the channel, you sit up on your board to catch your breath. You look at the frothy area of flotsam and jetsam where the waves are still unloading and are surprised to see no sign of Nelly yet. You look for him further inside, but don't see him there, either.

135

You look back outside anxiously. You realize you'll have to do better than you just did if you're going to win this contest. Suddenly the air horn sounds the end of the heat.

You can only hope now that Nelly gets disqualified for interference. As for Jacala Boy, it's unlikely he'll score higher than you. You see him on the beach as you head up to the grandstand. He makes a fist at you.

"And the second place winner is . . ." the announcer calls, "Jacala Boy Bones!" Clapping and hoots fill the air. "And first place goes to . . . Nelly Yater!" Amidst the cheers, the announcer reveals that you've been disqualified.

The End

The End

An avalanche of whitewater rumbles behind you—it's at least sixty feet high. You lower your stance and shift your weight forward to try and outrun it.

Unfortunately the board you're riding has an odd shape. It's not designed for down-the-line speed, and as you slow down the mountain of whitewater mops you up.

Your arms and legs get wrenched in all directions. Then you get tossed to the bottom and dragged, then bounced between massive coral heads. You feel like an underwater pinball in Neptune's kingdom of games.

You wait for the violent rush of water to let up, but it doesn't. Alas, you inhale a deep gulp of water. It rushes straight to your lungs. Your chest goes into spasms. You can't breathe water. You're only human.

On the beach, you're swarmed over by medics and media. "Could you ever have imagined this would happen to you in the most important heat of your career?" a reporter asks.

"To be honest," you reply matter-of-factly, "No. When I train, I think only of winning. This is a big upset."

The medics determine that your wounds need more serious attention, so they bring a stretcher down to the beach and lift you onto it. As they carry you off, a news reporter walks alongside you with a camera, asking why Jacala Boy didn't help you in.

"Jacala Boy Bones helped me a lot out there," you respond coolly. "I told him I'd make it in on my own."

Just then the audience erupts in cheers—Jacala got an amazing ride. You lie on your stretcher, totally bummed. You lost in a big way.

The End

The End

You turn the Jet Ski sharply down towards the trough, and just miss Tita as she pulls up into the barrel. The wave detonates behind you like a military bomb, annihilating everything in sight and sending an explosion of whitewater a hundred feet into the air. A fifty-foot wall of whitewater rumbles in your wake. You gun the Jet Ski and outrun the maelstrom. As you angle for the channel, you see Tita pull out of the humongous barrel. She launches off the back and glides through the sky, blowing you a big kiss. Not long after she splashes down, you pick her up, then head towards shore.

Throngs of cheering spectators meet you on the beach. Tita lifts you onto one of her shoulders and carries you to the grandstand. You take the stage beside the injured Jacala Boy and the hard-bodied Yater. When Nelly is announced as taking second place, your win becomes certain. You leave the stage with your $500,000 check in hand, but Tita blocks your way. "Half of that money is mine," she says, and she is dead serious.

Another giant droplet of water falls and hits you squarely in the chest. You lose your balance, and get thrashed as millions of gallons of saltwater drive you to the reef below. You try to remain calm while in the violent washing machine. But you get wrenched like a cloth puppet in a dog's mouth, and you begin to panic. As you panic, you struggle and use up the little oxygen left in your lungs. You calm down and go into Zen mode as life starts to end.

Tita Hulkington, still on the Jet Ski, races this way and that over the flotsam, searching and calling your name. When the next set roars forth and you do not emerge, she rides back towards the channel.

From the beach, Jacala Boy hears about your fatal wipeout and gives his last regards: "Ho braddah, you wus full on."

The End

The End

You reach the light in the wall and swim through the crack. You make it to the other side and see the sun shining through the surface some thirty feet above. You put a foot on the coral wall to push off towards daylight.

Suddenly, the crazy man's hand reaches out of the crack and grabs your leg. You try to kick him with your free leg, but you kick right into a protruding coral head and cut your foot severely. You grab onto the gnarled walls and force yourself out of the crevice.

It's a tug-of-war. The man's strength surprises you. You look back and see his pale face, then notice a rope tied around his waist, anchoring him back to his den. The rope won't give, and he won't let you go. Pain shoots through your calf as he bites a chunk out of it. You scream, your precious air escaping you. He drags you back to his den. This is his meal time and not your Miller time!

"No one mess with Da Hui," the gang leader says. "You goin' down now, stranger. C'mon boys!" he shouts, then his North Shore battalion close in.

You look up at the circle of burly, tattooed bodies bearing down on you and become terrified. You try to dodge between two of them but are thrown to the sand. The huge men stomp on you like angry giants. Soon you hear your ribs cracking and your breathing becomes wheezy. As your internal injuries become ever more severe, you try to yell out for help, but only manage a faint whimper. When your assailants begin to kick at your head, you realize they intend to kill you.

"No . . . no . . ." you wheeze as you try to cover your head. Your ears begin to ring and the bright sun begins to strobe black.

"You lose, stranger," you hear a thug say as he stabs a knife into your kidney. He withdraws the blade, and they all run as you die.

The End

a)

You push through the pain as you glide up into the barrel. There's an immediate release of pressure on your foot as you tilt your rail to the other side to better ride the tube.

You exit the wave totally energized and paddle back out, confident that your foot will hold up for one more ride. But then you hear the air horn sound the official end of the contest.

Your scores are raised above the judges' box—that last ride garnered some high scores, one being a 9.8!

Jacala Boy and Nelly paddle in a few minutes later. Not only are you first to the grandstand, but you win the contest! It's a narrow victory, with Nelly coming in a close second and Jacala Boy not far behind him in total points. But you've won! Congratulations!

139

You quickly agree to Gavin's offer. "It's all down to the final tally then," you say.

As you make your way to the grandstand, some medics are helping Jacala Boy up the stairs. He looks pale and dizzy from his head injury. You squeeze around them, then bound up the stairs. Your foot slips and you land face-first on the top step, knocking out your two front teeth. You hold your teeth in your hand as blood pours out of your mouth. Then the announcer begins, "Second place goes to . . . Jacala Boy Bones!" Cheers erupt. "And first place goes to Nelly Yater."

While champagne sprays up at Nelly, a judge escorts you off the grandstand. You have been disqualified. You've lost your teeth, seven million dollars, and the contest. No smiling for the cameras today.

The End

The End

They begin by announcing the second place winner—Jacala Boy Bones. The crowd claps reservedly. JB gives you stink eye, then steps back out of the limelight.

"And now," the master of ceremonies says excitedly through the microphone, "the winner of the Pipe Masters event and the world title is . . ." You watch him intensely, praying your name will be called. ". . . Nelly Yater!"

The crowd erupts in jubilant cheers as Nelly steps forward and raises his fists high. "Yes!" he shouts above the fanfare as bottles of champagne are uncorked and sprayed over his head and he is handed a giant $500,000 faux check. You fade back into the shadows, blaming your loss on your "modified" board.

140

- -

You arrive on the beach, followed by Nelly. Jacala Boy needs assistance from the water patrol and arrives minutes later. As you strut up towards the grandstand, some die-hard fans ask for your autograph. But it's Nelly who is surrounded by journalists and photographers, not you.

Jacala Boy Bones gets some consolation from locals and family members as the medics attend to him. He soon takes his place onstage, a white bandage wrapped around his head.

"After this," he says to you. "I'm gonna beat you down."

You laugh at his threats. When the scores are finally announced, you garnered the most points overall. The announcer's voice blares through the speakers: "Ladies and gentlemen, the leading contestant has been disqualified for unsportsmanlike behavior towards Jacala Boy. First place goes to Nelly Yater!"

The End

a)

Medics immediately rush up to you on the beach. They lay you down on a large plastic sheet and go to work on your leg. The media gather around.

A few minutes of pain go by, then a medic says: "Your leg is stabilized, and we've got a good wrapping on it. You can keep competing if you feel up to it. Another twenty minutes shouldn't make it worse."

You look up at your shaper and sponsors, who have breached the media circle, and say: "Get me a new board—a longer board with more rocker. I'm going back out there to win the world title!"

The audience erupts in cheers as you get to your feet. You're handed a fresh stick, and you paddle back out. To the chagrin of your competitors, you immediately pick off a good wave from right under their noses. You score well, then take your position back out in the lineup.

141

The necklace is heavy, but you manage to swim through a crevice in the wall and up towards daylight. You remember the coordinates of the crevice by spotting the position of three tall palm trees on the beach relative to a house behind them.

You casually backstroke towards shore, the heavy jewel rising and falling on your chest with your breathing. You don't see Jacala Boy anywhere and can only assume that the contest has ended. You see some water patrolmen buzzing around on Jet Skis. You're glad they haven't spotted you. You want to keep your find a secret, lest the whole greedy world descend upon your treasure trove. To your relief, the water patrol soon head further up the beach. You angle further west for cover.

b)

The End

"And the second place winner is . . ." the announcer says. You pray it won't be you—you want the world title. ". . . Nelly Yater!"

The audience applauds as Nelly bows resignedly.

You and Jacala Boy listen breathlessly for the first place winner . . . When your name is called, you let out a cry of joy! Security guards hold the frenzied masses back and repel some water patrolmen who come at you menacingly.

"You guys are a liability!" you shout to the water patrol.

The cameraman who took your picture in the barrel screams that the shot is worthy of a dozen magazine covers! Congratulations!

142

- -

Tita Hulkington races you to the beach, then lifts you onto her shoulders and marches you up to the grandstand amid a roar of cheers. An injured and aggravated Jacala Boy lumbers onstage beside you, while Nelly is carried up by some of his admirers.

"In second place . . ." the loudspeakers blare, "Nelly Yater!" When you're announced as the winner, you throw up your fists in triumph.

Suddenly Jacala Boy pushes you down and says: "You a cheater!"

"Hey!" Tita interjects, jumping onstage and slamming JB up against the grandstand wall. "My tow partner won fair and square, so back off!"

JB is terrified and apologizes to Tita. You and Tita crack open some beers. It's St. Pauli Girl time!

The End

The End

"Who are you?" you ask the crazy-looking man. "What do you want?"

"Food!" the emaciated cave dweller replies, then lunges at you with the surfboard skeg, cutting into your neck.

You push the madman away, but he lunges at you again and buries his teeth deep into your shoulder.

"Aaaah!" you howl in pain as he bites a chunk from your shoulder. You kick him in the crotch, and he stumbles back.

You're drenched with blood and about to pass out. You fall back against a coral wall. The maniac comes at you again with the surfboard skeg. He soon overpowers you. Then he puts on a grimy bloodstained bib.

143

"G'day, mate," says the sharply dressed man with an Australian accent. "Allow me ta introduce meself. Me name is Gavin Bishop, CEO of Power Plays sportswear. Have ya heard of us?"

"Of course," you answer. "You're the top brand in Australia, last I checked."

"That's right, mate. Still are. Ya know, I was really impressed with yer surfing out there. Yer grace-under-pressure and rebel-under-threats presentation would work perfectly for me company, so I'd like for ya ta represent us."

"Me represent you?"

"Of course, we'll be representing ya as well, if that's how ya prefer ta put it, mate. I can offer ya seven million the first year alone . . . But there's a slight catch. Ya gotta win here today."

b)

The End

The next day, you're still in the hospital. Your head is shaved on one side and a gruesome row of stitches marks where it was sliced open. You look out the window at a striking view of the Crouching Lion rock formation and some dramatic eastern gullies.

An attractive nurse walks in and takes your pulse. The nurse caresses your arm while administering medicine.

"There's someone here to see you, but after they're gone," the white-capped hottie says in a whisper, "it's time for your sponge bath."

Those words bring you rising excitement. But then Jacala Boy enters the room and you're stricken with fear. You scream out to the nurse, but to no avail. You're alone with the burly Hawaiian.

"You make Jacala Boy lose, brah," he says. "Now wot you gonna say 'bout it!" He takes a scalpel and cuts off your tongue, silencing you forever.

144

Jacala Boy shoots his board up at you. It comes close to piercing your side, but you're able to catch it in mid-air. You hold onto it as if to prove you're above his saboteur tactics. But suddenly, the leash pulls taut from Jacala Boy's ankle and you are immediately slung back into the pit and worked severely. Your equilibrium goes awry and you can't determine which way is up. You're held under for so long that you begin to panic. Will you run out of breath?

b)

Heads - Page 88a **Flip a coin** **Tails - Page 105b**

The End

You walk off the stage's side stairs, letting Jacala Boy gloat in his win amid the roaring fanfare. Ironically, you bump into the cameraman who caused you to lose the contest. He looks shaken up, but you feel no mercy or remorse. You have the urge to punch him right here and now.

Your brows grow angular as you grab him by the collar and demand: "So what do you have to say for yourself, bulb head?"

"Look at this!" he says, showing you a digital image on the back of his camera. You loosen your grip. The shot he got of you in the tube, just before you ran over him, is absolutely amazing.

"I've already showed it to three surf mags," he says, "and they all want to consider it for their next cover. You may not have won the contest, but this photo might bring you more sponsor money and new contracts."

You throttle the Jet Ski and are able to crash through the pitching lip to safety. The back of the wave is twenty feet high in itself—a harrowing sight to witness as you race to catch up with Tita Hulkington. Seconds later, she glides over the top of the humongous comber, having ridden a cavernous barrel.

"Yeaaaaaah!" you hoot ecstatically as you pull up beside her. She tilts the big-wave board up to you, which you stow on deck as she climbs astern the Jet Ski. You race back to Pipeline beach, then saunter up towards the grandstand amidst great fanfare.

Tita stops short and says: "This is as far as I go. Good luck."

You smile and squeeze her cheek, then continue to the grandstand. An injured Jacala Boy meets you there, as does Nelly. The fanfare simmers as the results are announced.

Nelly takes second place, and you take first. It's Miller time!

The End

The End

You're still feeling queasy as you sit in the lineup next to Nelly. The beating you took would have kept most riders on the beach, but Johnny Daring's encouragement and your drive have got you back out to finish the heat.

With only seconds left in the contest, you outjockey Nelly for the first wave by paddling deep inside. You get into the hook and spring to your feet, forcing Nelly to back out. You shoot to the bottom and turn up towards the crystalline lip cascading beside you. As you ride the Pipeline cylinder, your adrenaline surge meets your nausea and vomit shoots from your mouth as you exit the tube. The air horn sounds the end of the heat. You wipe the puke from your lycra jersey and face. Nelly didn't catch a final wave. You paddle in together.

When the scores are tallied, you just win over Nelly. Now, you have the world title, and a new nickname—Upchuck!

146

You are carried more than a mile by the currents, but you make it to the beach at Chun's reef. As you are about to get out of the water, you see a few surfers place their boards on the sand and begin waxing up. You quickly take off the necklace and latch it around your waist like a belt, then lift your trunks up over it. It's the prefect cover. You hustle up the beach, a great mound bulging at your crotch. You run into a Samoan, who smiles as you waddle by. You quickly cut alongside the road towards Pipeline. You stop at your Jeep to stash the necklace, then sprint the rest of the way to the contest site.

The contest area is somber. People are convinced that you've drowned. But when your arrival is announced, there's wonderment, and then soft applause, as though people think they're seeing your ghost. The master of ceremonies tells you over the loudspeakers that Nelly has won the contest and you came in third. You smile humbly and your crotch is sore, but your mind is focused on how you will score big booty in the coming days.

The End

a)

"Aloha," the man says with a kindly smile.

"Johnny Daring?" you ask. "Nice to meet you!" you say excitedly, pushing the medics away. As you stand up, you step on broken glass and slice your foot. You mask your pain and manage to stand firm.

"You know," the 1970s Pipeline surfing legend says, "I've popped my eardrum, drilled my stick into the reef, and twisted my foot any number of times. Guess how I knew when I could surf again?"

"I don't know," you reply, a bit discombobulated.

"When I could stand firm," he replies, then signals to one of his companions, who hands you a new board. "Sign on with me, with Pipecleaners," Johnny says, "and I'll take real good care of you."

You take him up on his offer, shining your shaper. You stroke back out and immediately get pitted in a spitting tube. You return to the lineup in ecstasy, but tensions are high.

147

You make your way towards the light and find a crevice in the coral wall that leads out. You swim through it, pushing along from one natural handhold to another. You're almost through the tunnel. The ocean surface is not far off. You're going to make it!

Wait! Your necklace snags on a protrusion of coral. You work to free the necklace, but that big diamond has wedged itself tightly into a crack. You could easily release the clasp, but you refuse to leave the precious diamond behind.

At last, you wrest the necklace from the coral. You are almost at the surface, but you're totally out of breath. You black out. Your valuable treasure carries your body to a watery grave.

The End

The End

At the hospital, you are injected with all sorts of painkillers and the doctor stitches up your ugly head gash. After surgery, a nurse straight outta heaven glides in with a bowl of steaming hot prune soup for you.

"Drink slowly," the nurse says with a mischievous wink. "After this, we can play doctor and give each other enemas."

The nurse is abruptly called out of the room, then Jacala Boy comes in and pulls up a chair beside you.

"I just come to say, kala mai ia'o—I'm sorry, brah," he says, his voice quavering a bit. "I interfered wid yo kine style. If not for dat, you make win contest, brah. Eh! We cool den?"

"Forgiven," you reply curtly. "Oh, and on your way out, can you send the nurse in with the bedpan, ASAP?"

148

- -

"Whoaaaaaa!" Jacala Boy screams as he gets hurled over the falls. He's encased in the lip you're trying to squeeze under, and just before you pull into the barrel, he reaches out and grabs your arm, causing you to fall.

You get hideously pummeled underwater. When you finally resurface, you're within five feet of the beach and your board is in two pieces.

Discombobulated, you stand up only to get smacked down by a powerful shore breaker. You look back over your shoulder and everyone is staring at you with their mouths open. You look down and realize that your bathing suit has been ripped off! You're naked! Your clothing sponsor throws you some new duds, but it's too late, you've already earned an embarrassing nickname. You sit on the beach and watch the water patrol pick up Jacala Boy. There's only seconds left in the contest. A man approaches you in a fancy suit.

b)

- -

Heads - Page 143b   **Flip a coin**   **Tails - Page 153b**

The End

You quickly agree to the executive's deal. After all, what do you have to lose?

You take the stage beside an injured and disgruntled Jacala Boy and a hopeful Nelly. JB whispers a death threat into your ear as the master of ceremonies begins: "I regret to announce that two of these three athletes have been disqualified for unsportsmanlike behavior. Jacala Boy Bones and Neil "Nelly" Yater, please exit the grandstand."

You practically faint. You've won it all!

"Congratulations," the wealthy exec says. "Yer now signed on and have just made yer first seven million. Furthermore, ya've found da magic bonus page in yer story. Go ta www.xpipex.com and click on da yellow sun ta claim yer special reward! Smile, mate, ya've found da coin-toss magic!"

The master of ceremonies takes the stage and announces: "In second place is . . ."

"Just a moment!" one of the judges calls down. "Hold the announcement!" A number of burly water patrolmen are arguing with the judges. After a few minutes of general confusion, two judges come down and speak with the announcer privately.

"Ladies and gentlemen," he continues, "I regret to announce that one of the contenders has been disqualified for endangering other riders and the water patrol."

When he calls your name, you explode in a screaming rage and are ushered off the grandstand. Jacala Boy wins and Nelly takes second. Ironically, a month later it is your tube ride (shot by the cameraman who got in your way) that appears on the cover of *Ocean Surf Magazine*.

The End

The End

Jacala Boy is late to the grandstand, and arrives with his head wrapped in white gauze. Nelly stands between the two of you, but that doesn't keep the burly Hawaiian from uttering pointed threats.

"Hey, back off," you tell him. "I could just as easily be mad at you for getting in my way, but I don't hold grudges. Competitions are fierce, and I do what I have to do to win."

He sneers back, "Beware of false crack medivac, brah!"

"Neil Yater wins the contest!" the MC shouts as exultant cheers erupt from the crowd. You're deflated, even as the MC says, "And Jacala Boy Bones is disqualified for unsportsmanlike behavior."

- -

Coming around the corner, you see a larger coral den with a pool of water at its center. The pool is perhaps six feet deep and the bottom appears to be covered with abalone-like shellfish, which are reflecting light from a crevice to the side.

Without wasting a moment, you take a deep breath and plunge into the glowing pool, then swim towards the source of light. You round a bend and swim up towards daylight. You reach the surface just when you can't hold your breath any longer.

The water patrol reach you minutes later on their Jet Skis, then zoom you to the beach just in time for the awards ceremony. You're surrounded by medics and reporters. The medics decide you're well enough to join Nelly and the injured Jacala Boy on the grandstand. Nelly Yater wins by a wide margin, and Jacala Boy takes third. You're happy to be alive and in second place.

The End

The End

Tita Hulkington whisks you into shore, adjusts her G-string, then walks you up to the grandstand. Nelly looks at you with a perplexed expression. He didn't see your ride. Jacala Boy, meanwhile, is being loaded into the back of a lifeguard truck.

"The second place winner of this year's Pipe Masters is . . ." the announcer begins, "Nelly Yater!" The crowd applauds reservedly.

When you are announced as the first place winner, the fanfare becomes deafening. Tita takes the stage and lifts you onto her shoulders, then you are handed an oversized $500,000 check. It's a bittersweet finale. After what happened to Jacala Boy, you did not expect a cheering crowd. Apparently, only you and JB know what really happened out there. Your Machiavellian win will forever weigh heavily on your conscience.

151

You surreptitiously watch Jacala Boy, who wears a confident expression. His look is disconcerting, given the fact that you totally blew your final wave—or, more correctly, the cameraman made you blow your last wave.

When the master of ceremonies announces Jacala Boy Bones as the winner, you watch him raise his hands exultantly before the roaring audience. Your near win—thwarted by the collision with the cameraman—begins to eat away at you like poison within. You vow to find the photographer and destroy all of his cameras. As for Nelly, he's basically gone. The six-time world champ has disappeared from the limelight, just like that.

b)

Heads - Page 145a **Flip a coin** **Tails - Page 154b**

The End

You make it to the light and swim out of the crack. You look up and see the sun shining through the surface some twenty feet above. You push your foot to boost off the coral wall, aiming for the surface, but just as you do, the lunatic lunges out of the crack and grabs your feet.

Enough is enough! you shout in your mind, then wriggle around and land a solid punch on his brow. He loosens his grip for a second—just long enough for you to kick away and swim towards the surface.

You break the surface nearing blackout. You see tingle bells as you breathe numerous deep breaths, but you soon get your wind back. You look down to see if the maniac is pursuing you, but all you can make out is an indistinct coral bottom. You wave for the water patrol, but the seas are heavy and apparently they don't see you. You swim towards shore, hoping not to get dragged down again.

- -

There's an incredible rumble behind you as a mountain of whitewater tumbles at your heels like an avalanche. You hold your line straight towards shore and squat for speed. Amazingly, the board you are riding seems to generate a speed of its own, driving ahead.

The torrent of whitewater eventually hits a deep spot in the reef and starts backing off. You're filled with a rush of relief as you realize you've outrun certain doom. You carve the reformed roller for hundreds of yards before racing down into a stunning inside bowl. After the ride you head for shore.

Even with his injury, Jacala Boy is the first to congratulate you on your ride, and when you end up winning the contest, you start celebrating with beers, then shots, then kava. You wake up with the hangover of your life, and because you blacked out, you can't even remember standing on the grandstand and holding the trophy. You've even forgotten your middle name.

The End

The End

Your alter ego, which you've been shunning for years—the part of you that wants anonymity—takes over. Amid the continuing fanfare and to the shock of the crowds, you grab a final surfboard from your old shaper and paddle back out. You ignore a cramp in your left foot and line up alongside a few anonymous Hawaiian locals. They congratulate you on your win with true aloha spirit.

You ride a few waves then paddle far out of sight, evading the media before coming to shore on an inconspicuous stretch of coast. The next day, you cash in your contest winnings and hop a plane to Texas for the sole purpose of evading the media and paparazzi. From there you clandestinely slip into Mexico, where you live, grow old, and die.

Some claimed to have spotted you there. They said you were a bum with long fingernails and ragged clothes, who surfed like a master and was always smiling.

You're perplexed. You look at the man, trying to make out his identity. "What's a matta?" your manager shouts in a high, droning voice. "Cat got ya tongue? What the hell are ya doin' here on da beach? Do you got any idea how much I got 'vested in ya?"

"Sorry, boss," you answer meekly. "I think it was my board."

"Bull crap!" your shaper says scathingly as he steps out from behind your manager. "We tested that board! Don't blame me for your failures!"

"C'mon guys," you protest. "I just got worked, okay? It happens."

"It happens," your manager mimics you in ridicule. "Well, dis just happens too. You're fired! Off da team!" With that, he tears up your contract. It's tough losing your main sponsor—tougher even than losing the contest. The incident makes you think about your life. You decide to go to India on a vacation. There you find a spiritual guru, Sai Bondukati. Years later you're still there, eating plain rice and levitating.

The End

The End

Trying to swim west becomes extremely tiring. A strong current pulls you back to the pounding surf just west of Pipeline. You crawl up onto the beach, and a crowd rushes to your rescue. Everyone sees your precious necklace and asks questions. You tell them you found the necklace floating on a piece of wood.

You take the stage beside your rivals and the results are announced to great fanfare. You come in second and Nelly wins, with Jacala Boy taking third. You care little about the results, because you're totally obsessed with the treasures you saw underwater.

That night, you organize a crew of three trusty helpmates. You plan to return to the site under the cover of darkness as soon as the hubbub subsides. However, a fanatical WWII treasure hunter sees your necklace on the news, goes diving at Pipeline and finds your spoils! Now the Japanese government and the state of Hawaii are suing you for the necklace and the treasure hunter for the return of the booty.

You walk off the side of the stage as Jacala Boy reaps the rewards of fame and fortune. You see the cameraman who interfered with you in the water. You call him an idiot then deliver a hard punch to his mouth.

He falls back onto the sand, his camera bouncing against his chest painfully. On the digital screen there's an absolutely amazing shot of you in the barrel. "Wow," you say, "that's a bitchin' shot!"

"Yeah," he says through bloody lips. "It could have made the surf magazine covers. It could have earned you contracts, fame, and fortune. But since you hit me, I'm going to delete it!"

And delete the picture he does. Unfortunately, he was right about its value. If only you had controlled your temper, that photo would have boosted you right back to surf stardom!

The End

Glossary

aerial ("an air") – a maneuver in surfing where the rider launches into the air, then lands again.

air horn – compressed air canister that emits a sharp horn sound when activated, used in most surfing competitions to mark the beginning and end of heats.

airdrop – to fall through the air with your surfboard still under your feet.

Aloha – Hawaiian for "Greetings" or "Be well."

amped – to be energized or excited to do something.

'aumakua – in traditional Hawaiian culture, a personal family deity, such as a shark, sea-turtle, egret.

back – the back of a wave.

backwash – outward-moving currents that collide with incoming breakers, causing the breakers (and sometimes the riders) to get bucked upward.

Backdoor (Pipeline) – a wave that breaks to the right off the Pipeline peak.

barrel – the hollow cylinder at the heart of a wave, formed by the falling curl. (See also: tube)

barrel-roll – to circle upside-down inside the barrel of a wave—a common bodyboarding maneuver, but one that is rarely ever attempted and executed in stand-up surfing.

beef – to fight, in Pidgin English. "Like beef?" means: "Want to fight?"

Bermuda trunks – shorts (or a bathing suit) that extend down to the knees or lower.

Bertlemann (bert) slide – to fling your feet and board out 180 degrees while doing a semi-layback. Invented by Larry Bertlemann, who hails from the Big Island of Hawaii.

bodyboarding – riding the surf on a small rectangular board made of foam. Used to be called boogie boarding.

boil – an upwelling of water, usually over a reef, sometimes used by surfers to mark the takeoff spot on a wave.

bomb – a big wave, or a wave that is bigger than most during a particular surfing session.

bombie – common Australian usage, short for bombora. A bombie is a wave breaking far offshore, usually over a deep reef.

bottom drops out – a wave whose trough suddenly becomes radically concave.

bottom turn – a turn performed at the base of the wave, aiming the surfer back towards the wave face, or "down the line."

bowl – a hollow tube section. (See also: inside bowl)

brah – Pidgin English for "buddy," "you," or "sir."

breaker – a breaking wave.

bull shark – an aggressive, unpredictable tropical shark known to attack humans.

bust – to bust a move: to attempt a maneuver. (See also: pull)

carving – to do rounded turns on a wave face.

caught inside – when a surfer is caught inside of breaking surf and pushed towards the beach by the currents.

cave – deep crevices in the Pipeline reef that surfers have been pushed into on wipeouts. (See also: hole)

chandelier – water falling in pieces at a barrel opening, threatening to bar the rider from exiting the tube.

channel – a pass, usually between two reefs, where surf typically doesn't break. Channels are used by surfers to safely approach a lineup, and by photographers as a safe vantage point from which to view the waves.

clean (surf) – smooth, glassy (not lumpy) water surface with esthetically balanced waves. (See also: glassy)

closeout/closing out – a wave and/or tube that does not taper evenly, but folds over all at once. (See also: shutting down)

Cloud 9 – a reef break in the Philippines that sometimes resembles Backdoor Pipeline.

cloudbreak – any wave that breaks far offshore, towards the clouds on the horizon. Cloudbreak proper is a world-famous wave located in Fiji.

coin-toss magic – a mystical part of the *Experience Pipeline* script that unlocks an electronic door, launching the reader on a real-life treasure quest.

comber – a wave before it breaks that rolls in slowly, "combing" the bottom contours, sometimes shifting shape.

coral head – a protrusion of coral that extends up from the reef, usually the shape of a cauliflower, ranging from three inches to twenty feet across, and dangerous to fall on.

cranking – when the surf is good and consistent. (*See also*: pumping)

Crouching Lion – coastal ridge rock formation on east Oahu that resembles a kneeling lion.

curtain – the falling lip of a wave.

cut back – to sharply turn and reverse direction while riding a wave; a turn performed to get back to the section of the wave that has the most push.

Da Hui – legendary North Shore legion of experienced surfers, waterman, and hardcore locals. Once possessing a fearsome, gang-like reputation, now slightly less organized but still commanding respect.

da kine – Pidgin English for "the best," or, referring to something as "that one."

deck – the top of a surfboard.

deeper – to be closer than other riders to the peak of a wave or its breaking curl. It is considered a violation in contest surfing to "drop in on" someone who is riding closer to the curl.

ding – a crack, hole, dent, or puncture in a surfboard.

double-up – when two waves or partial waves merge into one, forming an extra-thick breaker.

down-the-line – when referring to a wave, means a fast, long, peeling wave.

drop in – when a surfer goes from a prone to standing position and rides down the face of the wave. Also, when a surfer rides down the wave in front of another surfer, cutting them off. Dropping in on people is considered poor etiquette. (*See also*: snake)

dry reef – when water is drawn up the face of the wave, coral can surface at the base of the wave, presenting a serious hazard to surfers.

duck-dive — when a surfer drives their board underwater with the strength of their arms and knees or feet. When performed successfully, the rider will emerge at the back of the wave and have some momentum to continue paddling forward.

epoxy — a type of resin used to coat surfboards, said to be lighter and stronger than traditional resin.

face (wave face) — the front or wall of a wave, extending from the trough to the crest.

fa'afafine — a Samoan man who dresses and behaves like a woman.

fait accompli — (French): an accomplished fact, presumably irreversible; a "done deal."

fakie — to ride a surfboard backwards with the fins in front and the nose of the board in the rear.

falls — the lip of a wave as it falls down, like a waterfall.

false crack — (Pidgin English) to hit or punch, as in to hit someone in the head.

false crack medivac — Pidgin English for "to beat someone so badly they have to go to the hospital."

faux check — giant poster-sized cardboard check handed to competition winners. The actual prize money is usually distributed in the form of a certified check or wired as a direct deposit.

First Reef (Pipeline) — the main Pipeline break, about fifty yards offshore, where the wave is most hollow.

fish — a "retro," short but wide surfboard, usually between 5'6" and 6'6" in length, that has the stability of a longboard but a degree of maneuverability more like that of a shortboard.

flats — the flat water in front of a breaking wave.

floater — a maneuver in which surfers glide on top of a barrel for a short period of time.

foam — the airy, bubbly water that is the aftereffect of a breaking wave. In big surf, the foam can be three feet deep. If a rider surfaces in this, they can be suffocated by it. (*See also:* soup) free surfing – to surf recreationally, free from contest constraints.

freefall – when a surfer falls through the air from high up on a wave, usually during a wipeout. (*See also*: airdrop, over the falls)

full-on – to the maximum extent.

glassy (surf) – waves that are so smooth, they resemble glass. Requires an absence of wind.

gnarly – highly intense and/or critical.

gun (big-wave gun) – larger surfboard made for paddling into big surf. Usually between eight and eleven feet long.

hairy (or hairball) – scary, dangerous, and/or difficult to negotiate. (*See also*: gnarly, heavy)

Haleiwa – pronounced "holly-a-vah." A high-performance surfing break fronting historic Haleiwa Town on North Shore. It is one of the three venues for the Triple Crown of Surfing competition, the other two being Pipeline and Sunset Beach.

hang loose – Pidgin English for "take it easy."

hang-time – the amount of time one remains in the air during an aerial, ollie, or while going "over the falls."

Haole – Hawaiian for a Caucasian, usually used harmlessly but sometimes pejoratively. Literal translation: "Person without a soul."

Hawaiian scale (wave height) – in Hawaii, waves are measured by their backs (as opposed to by their wave faces, which is the case in every other part of the world). A wave that has a ten-foot face would be called a five-foot wave in Hawaii.

heat – one round in a surfing competition, usually lasting between twenty and forty minutes.

heavy – powerful, ominous or extreme. A potentially consequential wave or situation. (*See also*: gnarly)

Himalayas – a low-key big wave surf spot on North Shore, far west of Pipeline, which gets big, dangerous, and sharky.

ho – Pidgin English for "hey" or "eh," such as in: "Ho brah, howzit?"

hold down – to be held underwater by a breaking wave in the impact zone, usually after a wipeout. A combination of tumbling water and heavy currents can make it difficult for a surfer to swim to the surface.

hole – a deep spot in a reef or sandbar. Can also refer to a current which holds a paddling surfer in place, preventing forward progress.

hotdog – to ride playfully and with skill, to show off.

Howzit? – Pidgin English for "How are you doing?" or "What's new?"

impact zone – the area where waves crash down.

in position – to be in a suitable place to catch a wave.

inside – refers to the area between a breaking wave and the shoreline.

inside bowl – a section of the wave (that forms after the wave peak has broken) towards the inside, characterized by a tubing section.

Jacala Boy Bones – often misinterpreted, hard to predict Pipeline local and contest minotaur. JB has one daughter and seven tattoos.

Jeff Clark – pioneer of Mavericks big-wave surf spot in Northern California.

Jet Ski – a brand of Personal Water Craft (PWC), manufactured by Kawasaki. (See also: PWC)

judges' box – a raised structure built for surf contests where the judges sit. The judges' box commands a clear view of the lineup and is often equipped with an overhead scoreboard, on which competing surfers and spectators alike can see the running tallies.

k den – Pidgin English for "Okay then."

kala mai ia'o – Hawaiian for "I'm sorry."

kava – a mildly tranquilizing drink made from the ground root of the pepper plant. It is drunk both ceremoniously and informally. Consumed in excess, Kava can induce a stupor of fatigue and forgetfulness.

kick out – to exit a wave by riding or hopping off towards the wave's back.

kneeboarding – riding a short and fat board on one's knees.

Kona winds – south winds that hit Hawaii occasionally in winter. (*See also*: trade winds)

kook – a derogatory term in surfer parlance that describes a fool or person lacking in surfing experience or etiquette.

launch ramp – what surfers call a formation of water that appears like a perfect ramp in which to launch an aerial from.

ledge – the top portion of a steep wave.

lineup – place just beyond the breaking surf where riders want to catch the waves. "The lineup" can also refer to all the individuals that make up a group out surfing. Example: "All the pros are out, it's quite a lineup!" (*See also*: takeoff spot)

lip – the leading edge of the wave that falls as a wave breaks. Also used to refer to the crest of the wave.

log – a longboard, usually a particularly heavy and/or old one.

lolo – Pidgin English for "crazy" or "recklessly brazen."

lull – a period between sets of no wave activity.

161

Lycra jersey – a thin, tight vest made of Lycra (also known as Spandex) that competitors wear in a surfing contest. Each vest is colored differently so that the judges can easily identify the surfers.

macking – big, as in "That's a macking wave!"

mahalo – Hawaiian for "thank you."

mahalo nui loa – Hawaiian for "thank you very much."

mainland – the continental United States of America.

maki – Hawaiian for "dead."

maki die dead – Pidgin English for "very dead."

make the drop – to successfully ride down the face of a wave.

Mavericks – big-wave surf spot in Half Moon Bay, California, pioneered by surfer Jeff Clark.

mini gun – a surfboard roughly between seven and eight feet long. Larger than a standard shortboard, but smaller than a big-wave gun, it's a "mid-range" board made for surf between approximately ten and sixteen feet.

moke – Pidgin English for big Hawaiian dude.

Moray eel – coral-dwelling salt-water eel with sharp fangs.

mushburger (or mushy) – a crumbling, usually slow breaking wave, as opposed to a fast and steep wave.

Neil "Nelly" Yater – six-time world champ who makes everything look easy.

North Shore – The North Shore of Oahu, the most famous surfing arena in the world. Home to numerous large, heavy surf breaks, such as Pipeline, Waimea Bay, and Sunset Beach. When big, it's an experts-only realm.

nose (of a surfboard) – the front or leading tip of a surfboard.

offshore (wind) – a wind that blows from land out to sea and often helps to create a more hollow wave.

off-the-lip (or: off-the-top) – a surfing maneuver: to go up the wave face and turn sharply at the lip of the wave.

'ohana – Hawaiian for family.

ollie – while surfing, to hop up into the air with your board still "sticking" to your feet. Requires advanced skill and dexterity.

onshore (wind) – a wind that blows from the sea toward the land. Usually creates crumbly, or poor quality waves.

out the back – further out to sea than the common lineup. (See also: outside)

outside – further out to sea than the established lineup. "Outside!"—when yelled by a surfer—means a wave or set is coming that is bigger than the average wave that has entered the lineup.

Outside Log Cabins – a big wave break on the North Shore that sits far outside of Pipeline.

over the falls – to fall down with the lip of a wave as it is coming down, much like falling in a waterfall.

pay your dues – to take some bad wipeouts in big surf, or to struggle greatly at a given surf spot.

pearl – while surfing, when the nose of the surfboard penetrates under the water's surface, causing the rider to go headfirst into the water as if they were diving for pearls.

penetration – the ability to go through the surface of the water during a wipeout. In high-speed wipeouts, riders tend to tumble or bounce on the surface of the wave.

phat – common slang for exceptional, impressive, or admirable.

Pidgin English – an English-/Hawaiian-/Portuguese-derived dialect spoken by longtime Hawaiian locals.

Pipeline (*also known as* Banzai Pipeline) – a left-breaking wave on the North Shore of Oahu. The site of the Pipe Masters event, which is the final contest in the Triple Crown of Surfing competition, the other two sites being Sunset Beach and Haleiwa. Pipeline has earned a reputation as one of the best but most dangerous waves in the world. The right-breaking wave at Pipeline is called Backdoor, and can be just as perfect as the left, but often less predictable and more dangerous.

pit – the base or trough of a wave.

pitching – when the crest of a wave throws out.

pitted – getting barreled, riding in the tube, entering the green room, etc.

planney – Pidgin English for "plenty."

pull – to execute a maneuver, such as "She pulled an air." (*See also:* bust)

pumping – describes consistent, big and/or good surf. Also describes the subtle rhythmic weight shifting that a surfer does to generate speed while surfing.

punch out the back – to bodily penetrate through a wave face, lip or trough and escape successfully out the back of the breaking wave. Surfers use this method to exit a closeout wave.

PWC – Personal Water Craft, such as a Jet Ski, usually able to seat two or three people. Surfers use PWCs to tow each other into waves, and lifeguards use PWCs to make rescues.

Queenie Bones – mother of Jacala Boy Bones and wife of Wiley Bones.

rail (of a surfboard) – the edges of a surfboard running lengthwise from the nose to the tail. Surfing "from rail-to-rail" means to surf radically off the rails, tilting steeply from side-to-side.

reef break – a wave that breaks over a reef.

reform – after a wave breaks, the swell energy can continue to travel forward and reform into another wave on its way to the beach. For example, on a big day at Pipeline, Third and Second reefs might be breaking, but surfers might choose to wait at First Reef, where the same swells that broke outside will continue to roll in, forming an entirely new wave at First Reef.

rep – representative, such as a sales rep.

retro – a design or style borrowing from bygone times.

rideable – a wave that can be surfed. However, this is not always a standard judgment – a wave that is unrideable to one person may be entirely rideable to another, depending upon their skill level, experience, attitude, and perspective.

riding prone – riding on one's belly. Once a surf contest has ended, all contestants must return to the beach by riding prone.

riptide – an ocean current that can carry you out to sea. Swimming parallel to shore may help you escape it. (*See also*: undertow)

rocker – the degree of the convex curve of a surfboard bottom. "More rocker" means a more curved, convex bottom, while "less rocker" means a flatter, more level bottom.

rogue wave – a wave that is far bigger than the biggest set wave of the day.

roller – a wave that rolls in for a long time before breaking.

rush it – to transition into the surf, or any activity, usually with haste.

Samoan – a descendant of the Samoan Islands, "the Cradle of the Pacific." Samoans and Hawaiian Samoans are stereotyped as having a large build.

scoring system – in surfing contests, scores of 0.00-10.00 are given to surfers based on their ride. At Pipeline, the most points are awarded for good tube rides. A wipeout, even at the end of a great tube ride, will negatively impact a score. There are usually between three and six judges in a surf contest, all grading a surfer's ride, and the average total of their score is what the surfer scores per wave. Thus, if one judge holds up a 7.0, the second judge an 8.0, and the last judge a 9.0, for that ride, the surfer will score 8.0 for the wave – the average. Typically, a surfer's three or five highest scoring waves are matched against his or her opponent's three or five best waves. Whoever scores highest, wins!

sea urchin – a spiky, ball-shaped reef dwelling crustacean whose infectious spines easily can penetrate one's skin and break off deep within the flesh.

Sea-Monkey – brand name for a small brine shrimp, *Artemia salina*, sold as a pet, with a plastic fish tank, in toy stores. To surf like a sea-monkey is to surf animatedly, with great energy.

Second Reef (Pipeline) – the next reef out from First Reef, about sixty yards further out. Second Reef starts to break when the waves are about twenty foot on the face, depending upon the tide.

set – a series of two or more waves.

shaka – the "hang loose" hand signal common in Hawaii, formed by extending the thumb and pinky while curling the other fingers down towards the palm. Is a sign of camaraderie and goodwill. To "flash the shaka sign" is to show someone else this hand-signal, often in recognition of a good deed, event, or as simple bonding.

shaper – one who shapes surfboards.

shifty – describes erratic, shifty, unpredictable waves.

shore break – waves that break close to shore or directly onto the sand.

shortboard – a surfboard between 5' 10" and 6' 6" in length designed for high-performance surfing.

shutting down – when a wave or section is not makeable because it is closing out. "She got shut down" means the wave did not allow the rider to complete her ride. (*See also*: closing out)

sick – (in surfer/skater lingo): of superb quality and/or gnarly.

sideshore (wind) – a wind that blows parallel to the shore.

single fin – surfboard with one fin, usually a longboard, but can be found in retro style boards and big wave guns.

skeg – the fin of a surfboard.

slab – a square-bottomed wave with a steep ledge, often breaking in shallow water.

slotted – to be slotted or in the slot means to be perfectly centered in the curving trough as the wave breaks. (*See also*: pitted)

snake – to drop in on another surfer who is already riding the wave. A "snake" is a surfer who is guilty of this breach of etiquette.

snowball – a "ball" of whitewater that forms deep within a barrel and tends to "roll" towards the cylinder's exit. A snowball can overtake a surfer who is riding too far back in the tube.

soup – ocean water churned up by wave activity.

spit – watery mist that shoots out of a wave's barrel, caused by intense air compression within the tube. A strong spit can blow a surfer off the front of his board.

sponsorships – contracts between surfers and surf product companies, in which the companies pay the surfer to use and advertise the company's products.

stall – to purposefully slow down while surfing. A maneuver used to prolong tube rides.

staying open – refers to a tube with an end that stays open, allowing a surfer to exit.

stick – surfboard.

stink eye – to give someone a cold and mean stare. (In Pidgin English: "bumb-eye.")

stoked – to be very happy, usually from a good turn of events.

stonefish – tropical fish with a poisonous venom that can be fatal if stepped on.

stringer – a thin piece of wood running down the length of the interior of a surfboard, making it stronger. Some big-wave boards are given thick and/or multiple stringers to reinforce them.

stuff – to prevent a surfer from making a wave by riding in front of him.

Sunset Beach – an often big, shifty right-breaking wave on the North Shore. One of the surfing venues in the Triple Crown of Surfing competition series, the other two being Pipeline and Haleiwa.

sweet – slang for really nice or desirable.

swinging wide – a wave that breaks to the right or left of the usual lineup.

tail (of a surfboard) – the rear (not bottom) of a surfboard. (*See also*: nose, rails, rocker)

takeoff – the moment when a surfer catches a wave and jumps to his/her feet.

takeoff spot – the place in the lineup or on a wave that is ideal for catching a wave.

tanks – Pidgin English for "thanks."

Third Reef (Pipeline) – the next reef out from Second Reef, about a hundred yards further out. Third Reef starts to break when the waves are about twenty-five foot on the face, depending upon the tide.

three-wave hold down – to be held underwater as three consecutive (big) waves break over you. An extremely dangerous predicament that is difficult to survive.

thruster – a fast and maneuverable surfboard with three fins, usually between six and seven feet in length.

tiger shark – a territorial tropical shark known to attack humans.

tingle bells – small gold and purple spots that appear before the eyes when holding one's breath for so long that the brain loses oxygen and is about to shut down. They are most commonly seen when the eyes are shut, and can occur after long hold downs. They are foretokens of death, meaning the surfer must make it to the surface and get oxygen quickly, or drown.

tita – Pidgin English for a large woman or "lady moke." (*See also*: moke)

tombstone – during a wipeout, a surfer can be held so deep underwater that his/her leash is stretched taut, pulling most of the board underwater so that only the nose portion is sticking up, like a tombstone.

top-to-bottom — when referring to a wave, "top-to-bottom" means the wave is breaking steep and not mushing, and most likely producing a tube. When referring to a surfboard or style of surfing, "top-to-bottom" refers to a style that emphasizes going from the trough to the lip of wave often, focusing on tricky verticalness as opposed to "down-the-line" directness or speed. (*See also:* down-the-line)

tow board — a small but heavy surfboard equipped with foot straps, specially designed for towing into waves behind a PWC.

tow rope — a sturdy rope with handles used to tow surfers behind a PWC.

tow in — to get pulled by a tow rope on a surfboard behind a PWC (Jet Ski) into a wave.

track-top — treaded rubber grip applied to the surface of a surfboard in place of wax, for traction.

trade winds — the usual northeastern sea breezes of Hawaii. "The trades" tend to increase throughout the day and subside at night. They blow sideshore or offshore at many North Shore surf spots, including Pipeline and Sunset Beach.

tri-fin — surfboard with three fins.

Triple Crown of Surfing competition — the final three contests of the yearly pro surfing circuit, which take place on the North Shore of Oahu at Haleiwa Beach Park, Sunset Beach, and Pipeline, in that order. A highly anticipated and publicized event that sometimes determines who wins the Surfing World Title.

try move — Pidgin English for "get out of the way."

try wait — Pidgin English for "wait" or "be patient." Hawaii is not as fast-paced and tightly matrixed as the mainland, so patience is necessary.

tube — the hollow cylinder part of wave, at the trough and under the lip. The tube is a desirable and high-scoring place to be riding at Pipeline.

twin fin — surfboard with two fins, popular in the 1970s. Can be fast down-the-line but not quite as maneuverable as a tri fin.

two-wave hold down — to be held under the water as two consecutive waves break over you. (*See also:* three-wave hold down)

undertow — a downward-flowing current. A strong undertow can be dangerous, dragging a person underwater. (*See also:* hold down)

Velzyland – reef break on the North Shore, which has an amazing right-hand barrel at two- to ten-foot faces.

Waimea Bay – famous North Shore big wave surfing spot, mostly ridden going right. Until the late 1980s or 1990s, "The Bay" was considered the biggest rideable wave in the world.

wall – the front of a steep wave. "Wally" means a wave that has a steep front or face.

walled-up – indicates a wave face that resembles a vertical wall, and sometimes refers to closeouts. (*See also:* closing out)

water patrol – lifeguards trained in First Aid, CPR, and heavy-water rescues, who provide water safety for surfing events.

Wesside – Pidgin English for West Oahu, considered the stronghold of traditional Hawaiian culture.

wiki wiki – Hawaiian for fast or speedy

Wiley Bones – husband of Mrs. Queenie Bones and father of Jacala Boy.

wipeout – an unintentional fall while surfing, often a dramatic one.

worked – to get worked means to get thrashed about, usually during a wipeout or when caught inside. "I'm worked" can also mean simply "I'm very tired and my muscles are sore," but this can be from surfing good waves all day, not necessarily from wiping out.

WWII treasure – the Japanese are rumored to have left stores of gold and precious treasures throughout the Pacific during World War II. Today, treasure-hunting fanatics go to great lengths to find the elusive spoils.

xpipex.com – *Experience Pipeline* funsite.

Yamamoto's gold – Japanese imperial treasures reputedly hidden in caves throughout the Philippines and parts of the Pacific during World War II by Naval Commander Isoroku Yamamoto. (*See also:* WWII treasure)

you (the reader) – a contender for the World Title of Surfing in *Experience Pipeline*.

Zen mode – in surfing, when wiping out or being held under for a long time, some prefer to go into "Zen mode," or to relax instead of fighting against the churning whitewater. This can be an effective way to ward off mental panic and conserve oxygen.

Acknowledgments

The efforts to get this book out have been great, and rest solely on the shoulders of a few intrepid souls: Paul Diamond, for his creative vision and publishing insight; Eric Holland, whose help and simple friendship has kept me on track; Sean Davey, for his amazing Pipeline photographs; Ryan Mcfarlane, with his keen mind for graphic design; Ben Marcus; the folks at Surfline, for sharing with us the Sport of Kings; Bill Haber, great philanthropist, producer, and father; John Seagrave-Smith, super-agent guru and marketing Fu Manchu; Rabbit Kekai, for sharing old-time stories of Pipe; Sean Stratton, for first flipping this around with me at Cloud Nine; and last but never least, salamat to my lovely wife, Janice.

About the author

Quinn Haber is a novelist, freelance writer
and photojournalist. His columns on surfing
have appeared in numerous international
and online publications. His books, as yet
unpublished, include a trilogy of travel
adventure novels and a work of historical
fiction set in Paris in 1889. For many years
he lived in San Francisco, surfing Ocean
Beach and working at a publishing firm. He
now works for the State of Hawaii, helping
children obtain free medical services. Quinn
and his wife live on the island of Oahu.